Woodland Terrors

The Cellar Door Issue #1

Also by Dark Peninsula Press

Negative Space: An Anthology of Survival Horror
Violent Vixens: An Homage to Grindhouse Horror

Woodland Terrors

The Cellar Door Issue #1

Edited by Aric Sundquist

Dark Peninsula Press LLC
Copyright © 2022

Paperback ISBN: 978-1-7349378-7-9
Digital ISBN: 978-1-7349378-8-6
Library of Congress Control Number: 2022947030

Compiled, edited and formatted by Aric Sundquist
Cover artwork by Mikio Murakami
Proofread by Elsa Linna, Joel Sundquist, and Jen Lammi

Published by:
Dark Peninsula Press LLC
Marquette, MI 49855
www.darkpeninsulapress.com

First Edition.

Table of Contents

Acknowledgments

I would like to say a quick thank you to all the authors in issue #1 who trusted me to edit and showcase their work: Daniel Barnett, Douglas Ford, Amelia Gorman, Scott Paul Hallam, Ai Jiang, Scotty Milder, S.R. Miller, Maggie Slater, and Mark Wheaton. Also, a huge thank you to Mikio Murakami for his excellent artwork, and to my small band of proofreaders and beta readers: Jen Lammi, Elsa Linna, and Joel Sundquist. And yes, for anyone interested.... I stole the name of this series from the movie *Donnie Darko*. I'm not ashamed of this fact.

#

Finally, I would like to say a huge thank you to Daniel Barnett, who graciously dedicated his time and expertise to helping me read through dozens of shortlisted stories for the first three issues of The Cellar Door. If you haven't already, pick up a copy of *Nightfall*, the first book in his ongoing horror series, the Nightmareland Chronicles. The series is one of the finest pieces of fiction I've ever read. And it's my pleasure to have Daniel as the featured author for the premiere issue of The Cellar Door with his outstanding novelette, "Pigfoot." Thanks for everything.

Now, let's begin...

Aric Sundquist
Oct 2022

Woodland Terrors

The dusk rapidly deepened; the glades grew dark; the crackling of the fire and the wash of little waves along the rocky lake shore were the only sounds audible. The wind had dropped with the sun, and in all that vast world of branches nothing stirred. Any moment, it seemed, the woodland gods, who are to be worshipped in silence and loneliness, might stretch their mighty and terrific outlines among the trees.

--Algernon Blackwood, "The Wendigo"

CIRCLES
Maggie Slater

That night, the haints came closer. I crouched at the bedroom window so just my eyes, my fingertips, and the top of my head were above the sill, and even then, I hid behind the cotton curtain as they crept from the woods and started running circles around the house.

Their heads flew past my window, and their footsteps thundered over the front porch. Sometimes they bumped into each other, or clipped their shoulders on the house and went spinning off like whirligigs, until they pulled themselves back into line. They tripped over their own feet, their own guts, and tripped over the haints ahead of them, like a bunch of dirty bone clowns. If I stuck my arm out the window, I could have slapped them in the face, and the thought made me giggle.

Some of the haints I knew. Aunt Rita ran by, throat torn and flopping from side to side, threatening to jiggle right off, while her teeth—long and sharp—went clickety, clickety, clickety with each thumping step. Aunt Grace, skinny as a skeleton and ribs all bloody, raced along holding her blackberry-covered hands like claws in front of her. Aunt Mary was with them, too, her guts dragging behind her like long tangles of yarn.

Behind them all, the old pines arched up into the starless sky. Daddy always said the woods around here were nothing to mess with, but I don't think he knew about the haints.

Behind me, I heard a rustle of sheets as Amy stirred. "Lara? What are you doing? It's almost three in the morning."

The preacher haint darted by, his scarecrow legs pumping beneath him. A touch on my arm made me jump, but it was just Amy, cradling her bulging belly. I hadn't even heard her footsteps on the floor, but Daddy always said Amy could walk like a cougar when she wanted to.

"You seeing things again? Weird things?"

"It's the haints," I said.

"Haints? What, like ghosts?" I thought she might laugh at me, then, the way the doctor always chuckled a little when I told him about the things I saw sometimes. Momma said he was just trying to put me at ease, but it always seemed like he just thought I was lying to him. Instead, Amy peered out the window, holding her back with one hand and leaning against the frame with the other. Her big belly under her white nightshirt brushed the windowpane.

Aunt Mary ran by again, and this time I swore she was looking at us. My skin crawled.

Tugging at Amy's nightshirt, I whispered, "Get down. They'll see us watching."

Amy got down, but she took me by the shoulders, turning me to look at her. "You're just having a fit, okay? It's not real. Remember what the doctor said? It's not real, so you shouldn't be afraid. Whatever it is, it can't hurt you."

"I'm not afraid," I said. "The preacher's out there. The Aunts, too."

"You see Aunt Rita out there?" Amy leaned forward and squinted. "No wonder you can't sleep."

That made me giggle a little, until I looked back at the haints. They were all still running and tripping over each other, but they were looking at us as if they were seeing us seeing them. I got a sick feeling in my stomach and pushed back from the window.

"Wait..." Amy frowned and leaned forward until her nose almost touched the pane. "Wait a second... I see... something..."

"You see them?" My voice came out a squeak. "You see the haints, too?"

Amy shook her head a little. "It's faint, but it's there. Shadows, maybe, only there's nothing to cast a shadow."

Thumpity, thumpity, thumpity, the haints ran, their faces flashing past the window, staring at us.

No, not at us. At Amy. I shivered.

"This is so weird," Amy said softly. "I really feel like I'm seeing something."

"I don't think we should look at them anymore," I said. "Come on, now, let's leave them alone."

The moonlight glowed through the window; the shadows of the haints flickered across the curtains. Amy leaned back, rubbing her arms to get rid of the prickling skin as she hoisted herself to her feet, cradling her belly.

"Can I crawl in with you for a while?" I asked.

Amy pulled back her covers, and I scooted up against the wall. When she'd climbed in and pulled the covers around us, I snuggled up against her back like I always did when I was scared or sad or lonely. I hugged her as best I could with her big belly in the way, and she sighed, already falling back asleep.

I nuzzled my forehead against the space between her shoulder blades. "You're gonna be a real good mother," I whispered.

Amy's chuckle resonated deep inside her. "Yeah? Well, you're going to be a wonderful aunt."

"An aunt?" I giggled. "Like Aunt Rita?"

"Heaven forbid!"

We both laughed at that. I was so warm and comfy snuggled up there in that tight space between her and the wall, I imagined I was inside her belly with the baby where it was safe and surrounded by Amy on all sides, like an Amy room, far away from the haints.

"I'm gonna show the baby everything," I said softly. "I'm gonna show her how to fish, and how to climb trees, and how to catch lightning bugs. And I'll play games with her, and let her win, just like Aunt Mary lets me win all the time. And I'll learn to sew like Momma so I can make her dresses, and I'll sing her lullabies at night so she won't be scared of the dark."

"Might be a boy," Amy murmured. "Go to sleep, Lara."

But when I closed my eyes, all I could hear was the haints running, running, running around the house, and even through the walls, I could feel them watching us.

11

#

The trees creaked in the wind like old men laughing as Momma set the old crib on the grass with a sigh and a thud. Dust wafted from the padding between the wooden bars. The sunshine was so bright it felt like sand in my eyes.

"There." She brushed her hands together. "A little wash, and it'll be good as new."

Amy sat on the cement step, a big paperback folded over her knee. She was wearing sunglasses so I couldn't see her eyes, but her mouth frowned at the crib. "Great."

"It'll be real nice to have a baby in the house. You thought of any names yet?" Momma lifted out the mouse-nibbled pad. "You know, if you or Lara'd been a boy, I'd have named you Josiah. Isn't that nice? Josiah? It was your Daddy's grandpa's name."

The wind took that moment to rip through the trees, and in the woods I heard a crack like snapping bones. Amy tilted her head back and stared at the clouds racing through the little circle of blue sky over us. Daddy had cleared this plot of land in the woods himself when he was a boy, and it was only just big enough for the house and a ring of grass around it. He spent a few weeks every spring beating back the saplings that kept creeping in.

"Stop it, Momma." Amy's voice was low and hollow with her head back like that; the ridges along her throat made me think of the haints. "Just stop it, okay? You can't have it both ways."

Momma clicked her tongue and shook her head, just like Aunt Rita. "Sometimes the hardest lessons have blessings mixed in to make them easier to bear."

Amy glared at Momma. "It wasn't hard to bear until I came home. You're the one who had Preacher Mike come by. You're the one who invited Aunt Rita and Aunt Grace and Aunt Mary to come over to gossip about it, and then didn't say nothing to defend me. You're the one always saying it's such a shame, such a disappointment, to anybody who'll listen."

"It *is* a shame!" Momma clenched the mattress pad in her hands, digging her nails into the plastic. She sighed and closed her eyes for a moment, like she'd just gotten a headache. "Lara, why don't you go down to the creek and play?"

"Why don't you let her hear what you *really* think?" Amy sneered at Momma. It was a terrible look.

Momma just gave me her no-nonsense face. "Lara. Go, please."

I ran to the front of the house, but Momma always said curiosity was one of my demons, so I snuck right back to listen. The woods were closer on the far side of the house, the branches overhanging the roof. The pine needles muffled my footsteps as I slipped up close to the back corner where I could hear but not be seen.

Momma's hushed voice said, "Don't you pull her into this. She doesn't understand."

"She understands more than you think she does." That was Amy, and she wasn't trying to be quiet. "She's not stupid."

I made a mistake glancing into the woods. The haints were there, way back in the shadows so all I could see were the whites of their eyes and their long, jagged grins. I bared my teeth at them, so they'd know I wasn't scared of them, and when the wind whipped up again, most of them fluttered off deeper into the brush.

"No, *you* were stupid," Momma was saying. "You're supposed to be a good example to her. Just *think* of what she's learning from you now! You had your whole life ahead of you!"

"My life isn't *over*." I heard Amy grunt, and when she spoke again, I could tell she'd stood up. "I'll find a way to make it work."

"You have no idea what having a baby is like. How it'll change you, how it'll complicate everything. You think I didn't want to go on to college? Didn't want to get out of this place and start over? I wanted it as bad as anybody, but once that baby comes, your life is gonna change, and there's no way you can even understand how much until it's here."

"You just want me to stay and let this goddamn place suck the life out of me like it sucked the life out of you!"

Then they really went at it. Momma and Amy had fought before, but never like this. I'd never heard Momma scream like she screamed now, and when I peered around the corner, I saw her hair all wild about her head, her fingers stabbing the air like knives, her back and neck hunched like the sick cat Daddy shot last spring. And Amy hollered right back, her face red and blotchy, her whole body shaking.

I ducked back around the corner when Momma glanced my way. Among the trees, the haints had crept closer again, right to where the sunlight faded, and their laughter roared like leaves in a storm. I plugged my ears, but could still hear them, so I ran to the front of the house.

The haints had made a path during the night, beating the grass brown and flat in a perfect circle around the house. Dead beetles, worms, and spiders glittered in the dirt. I walked along the side of the trail, careful not to touch it, until I reached the spot where the haints had jumped from the ground to the porch. If they came any closer, they'd be inside the house. I glared into the trees, where they stood grinning and waiting for dark.

"You stay away from my sister!" I shouted, but they just kept staring, and I felt a little shiver run up my back.

I went right up to the edge of the woods and hissed at them. Their bulging eyes rolled in their skulls; their teeth clackety-clacked like they were laughing again.

I wasn't sure what would happen if they got inside, but I knew I didn't want them anywhere near Amy. So I started setting traps.

First, I moved the furniture on the porch so they'd trip over it if they came any closer. Then I took Momma's knitting yarn from her bedroom closet, and strung it up like a spider's web between the porch posts, tying the knots real tight. In Daddy's old woodpile, I picked out the spikiest sticks and put them at the edge of the porch so anything that tried to come around that way would get stabbed and die.

I was just stringing up Momma's knitting needles so they'd jangle a warning if anything touched the trap, when I heard a little gasp and found Momma standing at the screen door. She had her hand over her mouth and was staring at my trap.

"Lara! What are you doing?" She tried to push the door open, but the yarn kept it closed. The needles jangled. She took a step back, hand to lips, shaking her head. When she talked again, her voice was real low. "Lara, take this down, now, before Daddy gets home."

14

"But if I take it down, I won't have time to put it back up again before—" I almost said before the haints came, but I knew better.

For the longest time, when I was little, I wanted so bad for Momma to see what I was seeing—not weird things like the haints, but nice things, like the angels dancing in the sunlight over the church steeple, or the owl people who used to perch in the old oak down by the creek—but whenever I did, she'd close her eyes and start talking about seeing the doctor again, so I didn't tell her anything anymore.

Momma watched me for a long moment, and her hand slowly drifted back down to her side. "I want you to take it all down," she said. "Now."

I looked at my trap, my stomach flopping. "But—"

"Are you in charge of this family?" Momma snapped. "Do you make the decisions now? Does everybody but Daddy and me get to do whatever we like? I said *now*, Lara!"

It was the meanest tone Momma had ever used with me, and it cut me right to the heart. I pushed my arms against my aching belly and tears pearled up in my eyes. "I can't, Momma!" I cried. "I can't, I can't. The haints'll get in! The haints'll get in and get Amy!"

Momma's hands started wringing in front of her, then she reached up and clutched her hair. "Jesus Christ," I heard her whisper. She was shaking her head again, first slow, and then faster and faster. There were tears in her eyes, too, all of a sudden. "I can't do this," she said. "I just..."

Then she turned away like I wasn't even there and went back into the house. I didn't like thinking I'd made her upset, so I went around through the back to find her, but Momma's bedroom door was closed. I leaned up against it, and listened to the soft, husky crying on the other side. I knocked, but the crying didn't stop, and Momma didn't answer when I called for her.

Amy came into the hall. She asked me if I was all right, and I told her about Momma wanting me to take down the trap.

"The trap?" Amy frowned at me.

I took her to the front door. It looked perfect from the inside. Nobody would ever be able to get through it. Haints or not, we'd be safe.

15

"I haven't done the back door yet," I said. "But I will once Daddy comes home, and then we'll all be safe."

"Oh, Lara."

Amy looked pale, and had both her hands wrapped around her belly as she leaned on the door frame. Then she shivered suddenly, and her eyes went wide. It was only because she looked down that I looked down and saw a trickle of blood running down her bare leg.

#

I never got the chance to trap the back door. That's how they got in. By midnight, the haints were everywhere. Most lurked in the living room and the kitchen, staring at nothing. The floors were slimy with all the blood and mud and twigs and leaves they'd tracked in.

Daddy, Momma, the Aunts, the preacher, and the doctor all stood in a ring around Amy's bed. They were all haints, now. Momma was as pale as a flayed fish, and her purple lips hung open, dribbling spit and blood as she wheezed and shook. Daddy's head was bashed in, and where his face wasn't streaked with grease it was puckered with cuts the size and color of leeches.

The Aunts and the preacher huddled in close, rasping and gasping like all that running around the house had worn them out. The doctor's eyes had got pecked out somehow; all he had were big, clotted holes in his face that leaked puss.

The stink filled the house and the flies buzzed like TV static, making it hard to think straight.

I stood at the half-closed door, staring at Amy's motionless toes between the preacher and Aunt Mary. They were fat and pale, like giant maggots peeping out over the end of the bed.

Then I heard it, cutting through the whining flies: a shrill, terrified shrieking, clear as cool water. The doctor haint clutched the wriggling, bloody baby in his boney arms. It was a boy, a little boy, and it made me sick to see a haint touching him when Amy lay so still. When the Momma haint saw me watching at the door, she turned, and I saw Amy's arm dangling off the side of her bed, her sheets drenched red.

Those haints all turned to look at me then, wheezing through their grinning teeth. Amy's sweet, tiny baby screamed and screamed and screamed, terrified and cold and lonely, and before I knew it, his screams had built up inside me and I let out a shriek that blew the haints back against the walls. They couldn't come into my house, those nasty, rotting haints. They couldn't have Amy's little boy.

They didn't move when I rushed them, rushed the doctor, and grabbed the baby from him, but they sure moved fast after that. They screeched and clawed at me with the bones of their fingers as I ran out of the room, ran out of the house, and into the woods.

The trees shrank away from me, like they knew they'd done wrong by letting those haints live among them, and I ran with the baby until my feet were bleeding and the sun was gone and the night breathed cold down our necks. Even then, I kept running. All night long, the baby howled for his momma, and there wasn't a thing I could do, so I just tucked him up tight in my shirt and held him close as I ran and ran and ran, and the woods let us by.

Sometimes, I saw haints in the shadows, but they kept well away from me now. I figured if I ran fast enough and far enough, I'd find a place where there weren't any haints, where someone could take care of the baby and keep him safe and warm and happy forever.

But everywhere I went, there were haints. They ran around every house, every town. Around the cities, they ran five lanes wide, and you could feel their footsteps thundering into the ground for miles.

And that's when I realized the whole world was just running a circle around the sun, and all the grownup people were really just haints disguised to look alive by daylight. Maybe Amy knew that, too. Maybe that was why they'd killed her: because she wouldn't be like them, wouldn't run those circles going nowhere.

So I took her sweet baby up into the forested mountains. The trees there feed us and clothe us and keep us hidden. And when Amy's baby cries in the darkness, I hold him close and tell him about his momma up in Heaven with the angels and remind him that as long as his Aunt Lara is with him, no haints will ever come near.

17

LADDERS
Douglas Ford

Rusty found the old ladder buried in the earth after the work crew's departure. Tripped over it, in fact, nearly killing himself. Only the top rung showed above the dirt, and when it caught Rusty's foot, it almost sent him headfirst into the remains of an old oak that had once housed a family of woodpeckers.

Rusty considered his own position one of solidarity with those woodpeckers. Like them, and the rabbits and the raccoons and the bobcats that had once lived on the lot, he too appeared destined to become homeless.

The foreclosure notices on his own house started arriving not long before the empty lot next door sold to developers, who quickly started clearing it to make way for the construction of a new home. The same thing happened everywhere else in his once heavily wooded neighborhood. Originally, the remoteness of the area attracted him, but eventually he fell in love with the trees and the wildlife. Now it all seemed poised to vanish. Like him.

"Motherfuckers," he said to himself between sips of beer. He walked over to the bulldozed clearing next to his house—the latest parcel of land to go. Across the street, a minivan pulled into the new house facing his, and an entire family poured forth. They all smiled and waved to Rusty.

Rusty returned the wave, but not the smile.

The driver of the van, a balding man who seemed to wear only polo shirts, stopped and called out to him. "We're getting a new neighbor, I see. Isn't it wonderful?"

Rusty didn't know the man's name. Like their houses, the neighbors all looked the same. He wondered where they kept coming from.

He raised his beer in a mock toast. "I'd say it's a fucking shame of epic proportion."

The neighbor's smile vanished briefly, replaced by an empty stare of confusion. No doubt he thought he had misheard. How could anyone object to progress, to development, to the rising value of real estate?

Rusty could. He had a file full of foreclosure notices for Exhibit A.

Bile rose in his throat as the neighbor's smile returned. Raising his hand in a farewell salute, the neighbor followed his family inside the air-conditioned interior of that new house which would, no doubt, look like the one about to take shape on the vacant lot.

When Rusty turned on his heel to look at the rest of the damage, he tripped over the ladder.

#

It made no sense. If someone in the work crew left behind a ladder, why would they bury it?

It didn't seem like a simple act of carelessness. Not that this would surprise Rusty. He expected no less from the callous idiots who didn't give a fuck about displaced woodpeckers. They did their damage, and why would they care if they left some hardware behind? But a buried ladder? Maybe he'd just found a small stepladder that some fat-ass stepped on, causing it to sink into the soft dirt.

But when he tried to pull the ladder free, it wouldn't budge.

It looked old, and its faded brown color caused it to blend in with the rest of the terrain. From a certain angle, it looked like a natural feature growing from the earth itself.

More curious now, Rusty went to his carport—a very modest structure compared to the giant garages attached to the newer homes—and returned with a pick and shovel, which he used to clear away the dirt around the ladder.

The day still had a good hour of light left, and the mindlessness of the work helped sober him and distract him from his own problems. But the more he cleared, the further he realized the ladder went.

Finally, he hit something solid with his shovel. Clearing more dirt away, he unearthed an irregularly shaped barrier made of rough material. The ladder twisted at an angle, extending down into whatever the barrier covered. Sensing a kind of hatch, Rusty tried to pry it away with his fingers.

That didn't do the trick, so he tried the pickaxe, and the barrier broke away into pieces, falling into a crevasse that opened beneath it.

Rusty stared into the gaping blackness. The ladder twisted, like a root that had grown sideways to accommodate the barrier, but it maintained the dimensions and form of a functioning ladder. It didn't look natural, but it didn't look manufactured either. A strange scent wafted from below—an earthy scent—with traces of what smelled like chemicals. Ammonia perhaps.

Maybe an old bomb shelter, he conjectured, or a hideaway used by bootleggers. Long ago, such renegades prospered in this region, way back before people paved over everything.

He needed to make a decision: go down and investigate, or try to cover up the hole with the remaining pieces of the hatch.

Rusty knew he should do the latter.

Start minimizing the amount of trouble he got into.

Nah.

Maybe he owed the impulse to the beer, or perhaps the fatalism that had come over him as of late.

First, he tested the ladder. If it originated during the Prohibition era, it might crumble beneath his feet. But its sturdiness surprised him. It supported his weight handily, though he couldn't quite determine the material. Something between wood and iron. He couldn't see what held it in place, but it seemed reliable, so down he went into the darkness.

Quite a distance, in fact.

The walls of the passageway narrowed around him. It occurred to him that he'd found an old well, or God forbid—an abandoned septic tank. In the dark, he reached out and touched what felt like limestone. Someone cut this away a long time ago, he guessed.

Before descending further, he needed a flashlight, so he crawled back up into the fading sunlight. When he emerged, he once more saw the neighbor across the street, still wearing his polo shirt and now using a hose to water his hedges. Again, the neighbor waved to him, but Rusty pretended not to see him and returned to his carport to get what he needed. When he returned, he noticed the neighbor was watering his driveway, oblivious to where the water sprayed. In truth, the neighbor was observing him and trying not to make it obvious.

"You're wasting water," Rusty said.

"What?" the neighbor answered, but Rusty knew he heard him just fine because he now aimed the water at the bushes.

"Don't waste water," Rusty said. "It's a precious commodity."

The neighbor laughed, as if he'd just heard a funny joke.

Rusty pretended to laugh back before saying, "Fuck you." Instead of waiting for a reply, he stormed back to the ladder, now armed with a decent flashlight. It felt good to say that to his neighbor, so he returned with a hop in his step. Normally, his knees bothered him, the result of dislocating them too often, but curiosity made him forget all about his pain.

All the way down, the ladder seemed to twist and vary in width, like something grown instead of installed. After about twenty feet, he came to a rounded-out cavern of rock and dirt. It proved just tall enough for him to stand, though the roots of long-dead trees dangled overhead. To see anything, he had to push them out of the way.

Definitely not a well or a septic tank. He thought again of the possibility that he'd found an old cache for liquor barrels. Yet the light from his flashlight revealed only roots and dirt.

Until he moved the beam to the northeast corner. There he saw it, the body of a naked man, encircled by the same twisting roots that hung overhead. It looked like someone had tied up a corpse and left it underground.

The sight caused Rusty to call out in alarm, the sound of his voice filling the enclosure. But the man didn't react to the sound. He continued to lie there motionless, eyes closed.

In his panic, Rusty revised his earlier conjecture: not a hideaway at all, but a tomb housing some sort of mummy.

Heart racing, he leaned closer.

The man's skin didn't look withered or decayed—it looked pink and healthy, like baby flesh. Not only that, the root system didn't seem to just grow *around* the body; at certain places, like the abdomen and groin, it seemed to grow *into* it, like a series of umbilical cords delivering nutrients to the slumbering form.

Besides the roots, there was something else.

Tiny gray worms.

At first, he made the mistake of thinking they were maggots feasting on the dead. But a closer look revealed that instead of consuming the body, the worms were secreting a fleshy paste. As if working in concert with the worms, the root's branches pulsed, reminding him of a scorpion flexing venom into the body of its prey.

More fascinated than afraid, Rusty leaned closer. His light revealed two other bodies just beyond the man—a woman and a child, both naked and connected by the same series of roots, their bodies host to the strange worms.

A term for this discovery formed in his mind: a *nest.*

As he pondered, he heard a sound close by, something moving in the dirt.

He moved the light to find the source of the sound, glimpsing the man's face. This time, he didn't just call out in astonishment.

He screamed.

Then he scrambled his way back to the ladder, dropping the flashlight in the process. He didn't bother going back for it, instead groping his way up the twisting ladder. His heart hammered as the climb seemed to take an eternity, but eventually he hoisted himself out of the hole and back onto the ground. Hurriedly, he threw the pieces of the broken hatch over the opening, along with handfuls of pinecones and mulch. Anything he could grab to place between him and what he found down there.

"Oh, my Jesus, oh, my Jesus," he said, over and over.

Down there, in the darkness, the man's eyes had opened.

Rusty sat on his haunches, staring at the rungs of the ladder sticking up out of the earth, and he didn't move until he felt certain nothing would follow him.

#

In the days that followed, Rusty did all he could to dismiss what he'd seen. He told himself that it was an illusion brought on by too much drinking. Still, he avoided going back to the lot, and besides, the construction of the new house proceeded quickly, covering any traces of the ladder.

The only person he tried to tell was Charlotte, his ex-wife.

She called him two days after his experience, so he still felt shaken. Thus, he struggled to process what she wanted.

"The check is late," she said, apparently for the third time.

After what he'd seen, money hardly seemed to matter. He could barely remember to eat.

"You remember the lot next door?" he said. "It sold, and they're building another house…"

He couldn't finish the rest. He didn't know how to say it. Worse, he knew what she'd say. Something about his drinking. Even worse: she might have a point.

"Still carping about crimes against Mother Nature? Trust me, the squirrels and tortoises will find a new place to go. They always do. I'm so sick of all this doomsday shit you buy into."

"It's not that," he said, irritated now.

"I'm not done. You act like nature is some benevolent enterprise. But it's not. It's nasty. It's worms and blood and death. Remember the carcass we found that one time?"

"Jesus," he said. "Not this again. Animals have to eat."

Just before Charlotte had left him for good, she stepped outside to retrieve the mail and came face to face with a vulture pulling strings of flesh from an enormous, dead rattlesnake.

"Yeah, and it would eat you if it could," she said. "Nature's just a malicious machine that's biding its time before it can figure out how to do us in. Just remember this: everything in nature wants to kill us. Give me air conditioning and computers and microwaves and processed meals any day. I choose those things. You've chosen something else, and that's why we could never live together again."

Rusty closed his eyes and rubbed his temples with his free hand. "You weren't always like this. At one point, you wanted to buy the property next door. Just to keep it from development."

"That's rich," she said. "You want to talk about why we didn't? Where's that money you talked about saving? And oh, yeah—where's my check?"

"Bet money's not a problem anymore."

Charlotte lived with a real estate developer now. The cause or symptom of her current disease, Rusty couldn't tell. Now she couldn't look at a tree without imagining how to chop it down to build a new auto parts store. Because that's what the earth really wanted: more steel and plastic.

"It wouldn't be," she said, "if you got your priorities straight and started worrying about practical things.

"How does the saying go? The check's in the mail."

"I'll bet. Why don't you go chain yourself to a tree?"

"You'd like that. Just so you could bulldoze it, along with me."

"Would I ever," she said. Then she hung up.

To cool his rage, he took a long walk. Not like he had a job to go to. He walked briskly and without direction, covering areas of the neighborhood he'd not seen in a while.

Everywhere he looked, new houses were going up, and he passed several bulldozers sitting in ravaged lots, just like the one next to his home. Every new house looked the same. Even the people standing outside watering their grass looked the same—the men with friendly smiles and glistening white teeth, the women with faces full of makeup.

When he passed one of the recently bulldozed lots, a tall pine drew his attention, mighty in stature and at least a century old. He worried about the fate it would suffer with yet another new house going up.

He stopped and gazed upon its magnificence, already feeling as though he should mourn it, when he noticed something else.

The rungs of a ladder sticking up from the earth.

A voice called out to him from the house across the street.

"It's sold already!"

Rusty turned to see the source of the voice: yet another perfect male specimen standing on a well-manicured lawn, water pointlessly flowing from the hose in his hand.

"What?" said Rusty.

"It's already sold." Then that smile that looked like all the other smiles Rusty saw on his walk that day. "It's a seller's market, you know. As soon as a lot goes up for sale, boom! It's gone that day. Best try your luck somewhere else."

Rusty returned his gaze to the rungs of the ladder, and a horrible notion arose in him. If he dug away at the earth around the ladder, he knew he'd find another *nest.* He shivered as that word came to him again. He wanted to believe more than anything that he'd dreamed the entire experience.

"I say," the smiling man with the hose said in a tone that suggested he wanted to sound forceful without making it obvious, "you'd best try somewhere else."

Rusty didn't answer. A vision formed in his mind—the man's face beneath the ground, entwined with roots and vines, his features formed from the defecations and regurgitations of a thousand worms.

Rusty turned and walked toward his home, and he didn't stop until the front door was locked securely behind him.

#

In the days ahead, every time someone cleared one of the quickly vanishing lots to build an ugly new home, Rusty found himself scanning the area. More often than not, he spotted the rungs of a ladder sticking out from the mulch left behind by the machines.

No attempt to even hide them, he thought.

Then he reminded himself about how he had tripped over the first one, and how they blended in with the land's natural features. Somehow, they *were* natural features. Now that he knew what to look for, he couldn't help but see them.

Once, at night, after he turned off all his lights to save electricity, a flashlight beam came through his front window. Immediately, he remembered the flashlight he had dropped when he went down into the nest. He never went back for it. Even if he still tried to convince himself that he imagined the whole experience, he'd have to explain away the missing flashlight. So, he laid there on his sofa, watching the beam of light move across his wall, telling himself that it probably came from one of the new house owners walking his dog in the dark and using a flashlight for safety.

Just not *his* flashlight. Not possible.

Completed in record time, the new house next door served to emphasize how dilapidated, how unkept, how out-of-date his own house looked. Its manicured lawn stood in contrast to how Rusty let his grass grow wild and unfertilized. Kudzu vines and palm fronds sprung up from the weeds that dominated his yard. The day after he watched the flashlight beam move across his wall, he looked through the back window and saw something moving through those weeds, which had grown over three feet high.

A raccoon or a rabbit, he assumed at first, but when Rusty saw its head, he nearly gasped out loud.

A Florida panther. Ragged, with one ear missing, ribs showing through its emaciated frame. Regardless, it still somehow possessed the majesty of a once dominant animal, now reduced to a desperate, endangered existence.

The animal looked set to bound away, when Rusty heard the unmistakable report of gunfire. The panther thrashed in midair—as if caught in an invisible net—and for an instant, a storm of blood and fur surrounded its body. Then it fell back into the weeds, its shredded body hidden from view.

Rusty made for the back door, not sure exactly what he intended to do. As he stepped out, a man met him from the direction of the new house, an assault rifle slung over his shoulder.

Rusty, who had not yet met his new neighbor, stared at the man.

"Afternoon," the man said. "Don't believe we've had the pleasure." Without offering a hand to shake, he introduced himself as Sam Manila, the occupant of that brand new house.

The sight of the man sent a chill through Rusty. Not just because of the weapon he carried over his shoulder, but because of his familiar face.

Sam Manila looked just like the man Rusty had found buried beneath the earth. Only now he wore a white polo shirt and checkered shorts.

"Maybe now you'll clean up your property," the man continued. "Can't see what's hiding in all these weeds. Dangerous not to know what's out there."

Rusty didn't reply right away. Instead, he waded through the grass until he found the dead panther. The bullets had torn off one of its front legs and obliterated its head. One thing was for certain: Sam Manila knew how to aim his weapon.

At that moment, two others appeared behind Sam, apparently the rest of the Manila family—a woman along with a boy around thirteen. Rusty recognized them as the two others he saw beneath the ground that day.

"You get him, Dad?" the boy said, a perfect imitation of a real person.

Because Rusty felt certain they weren't real—not in the same way he considered himself real. Somewhere in his chaotic thoughts, he heard the voice of Charlotte telling him that people couldn't really exist in harmony with nature. Loving nature made no sense since it couldn't—and wouldn't—love you back. Given the chance, it would fight back and destroy you.

But would it do it this way? By birthing replicas of people? As replacements? For protection?

Sam Manila kept his eyes on Rusty as he answered the boy. "I got him good. That creature was a nuisance—not even designed for survival. Just useless skin and bones. I was reminding our neighbor here about how he needed to tidy up his property. Cut back some of these vines."

"Any form of nuisance could hide in there," said the woman. "Things like rats. Rats attract panthers."

"You don't want me to get attacked by a panther," asked the boy, "do you, mister?"

"He sure doesn't," said Sam Manila. "Do you, neighbor? You don't want any of us to get attacked by a wild animal. It's them or us. Isn't that right?"

Rusty didn't answer. His blood had gone cold, frozen in his veins. Sam Manila withdrew the rifle from his shoulder. Rusty shifted his weight, not sure what the man intended to do.

It turned out he only intended to hand the weapon to his wife. She held it and watched Rusty thoughtfully as Sam Manila began working something out of his pocket: the flashlight Rusty dropped when he'd disturbed their nest. He held it up for Rusty to see.

"They found this on our property. My guess is you dropped it there."

Rusty shook his head. "Not mine."

The man raised his eyebrows. "You sure?"

"Positive," said Rusty.

Sam Manila seemed to consider this. Then he used the flashlight to point at an old oak that grew wild and untrimmed on the edge of Rusty's yard.

"That needs to come down," said Sam Manila. "It drops leaves onto my backyard. I've got better things to do than to rake them up."

Mrs. Manila said, "He needs to play with his son and make love with me."

The barrel of the rifle inched close to Rusty as she spoke these words.

The boy nodded. "We like to play ball and eat hot dogs. You got a kid to play ball with, Mister?"

Rusty shook his head.

"That's a damn shame," said Sam Manila. He put the flashlight back into his pocket. "Do something about the tree. I have a good yard guy if you can't do it yourself. He'll dispose of that creature for you, too. You ought to do it soon, before the worms get to it."

Without saying any more, he smiled in a neighborly way. Then the three turned as one and returned to their house, where presumably, Sam Manila would make love to his wife and play ball with his son.

#

Later, after considering his lack of options, Rusty called the state's Wildlife Protection Office to report the murder of the panther. He kept his voice low, as if Sam Manila and his family sat crouched outside his front door, secretly listening.

After remaining on hold for over an hour, Rusty finally reached an exhausted-sounding person who simply said *hello* without introducing himself or announcing his department. When Rusty said he wanted to report that an endangered panther had been shot on his property, the beleaguered man asked him to repeat himself. After the second iteration of the event, the man said, "Let me get this straight. You're calling to confess that you shot a Florida Panther? They're endangered, you know."

Rusty breathed deeply and tried to conceal his exasperation. "Not me. My neighbor. He had what I think is an A.R. 15." Rusty didn't know guns, but he'd heard about this one on the news and thought it would grab his listener's attention. "He shot it in cold blood."

"Hold on," said the man. It sounded as though he set down the phone to talk to someone else. When he picked it up again, he said, "How do you know it's a panther?"

"I asked it and it told me. Jesus Christ, it's got four legs, tan fur, and big teeth." When he got no reply, he added, "Well, about the teeth, I'm speculating. My neighbor practically shot its head off. He's not..."

Rusty didn't know how to finish the sentence. He's not what? Real? Human? He could say *not natural*, but that didn't seem accurate. Not with what seemed like an increasingly inescapable conclusion: that nature had accomplished some kind of strange adaptation beyond his ability to fathom.

"He's not *right*," said Rusty, finally.

"What's your address?" said the person on the phone.

Rusty told him. Once more, the man put him on hold so he could talk to someone else. Standing near his back window, Rusty could see the place where the panther had died. A cloud of insects hovered over the area, feasting on blood and spoiled flesh. Overhead, he saw a dark speck. A vulture, he realized. Soon, more of them would appear. The cleanup crew.

And down in the dirt, Rusty knew, the worms had begun to eat. Raw material to use for later, probably.

30

The voice returned.

"We already have a note about that address. Are you the new occupant?"

"I'm the current owner," said Rusty. "What does that matter?"

The man didn't excuse himself before speaking to someone else. Rusty tried to hear the muffled conversation, but they kept their voices too low. When the voice spoke again to Rusty, it said, "Do you have weapons in the house?"

"I don't even hunt. Look, I think you ought to know what's happening here. I keep seeing people who aren't natural. I know this sounds ridiculous, but it's the truth."

"They're perfectly natural," said the voice. "Am I to understand that you have no weapons? Not even, say, a large machete?"

A wild thought came to Rusty. "You're saying I should get something to defend myself. You're saying I'm in danger."

The voice went silent. Rusty held his breath, straining to hear any muffled conversation. Nothing, until the voice resumed, enunciating each word carefully. "Just stay where you are. Someone will be there shortly. I'd like your assurance that you won't be any trouble."

"Trouble?"

"There are notes in your file. Also, something about a foreclosure."

Rusty hung up the phone. He checked the number, verifying that he had dialed correctly. Then he went to the front door, making sure he locked it securely with the deadbolt.

No sense in making it easy for them to get inside.

Through the front window, he saw his neighbor across the street, once more watering his driveway and staring blankly in his direction. If he could see the new house next door, he knew he would see them standing outside as well. Everywhere in the neighborhood, they knew about him. They knew that he knew.

He retreated to the back window and saw the vulture slouching toward the panther's carcass. "Go away," he shouted at the window. "Just get away!"

He couldn't explain the terrible anger he now felt for the vulture. It only did what nature created it to do.

31

Of course, the same could be said about the neighbors about to descend on his house.

If he couldn't prevent his own fate, maybe he could do something about the panther's. It now seemed incredibly important to do something. Anything.

Despite what he told the man on the phone, he did own a machete. With it in hand, he ran toward the vulture now sitting atop the dead panther, prepared to decapitate the horrible bird if necessary. But it bounded off before he could land a blow. From a distance, it glowered at him for interfering with its natural function.

Still, Rusty was determined that he wouldn't surrender the carcass to it. He would bury it instead.

Using the same pick and shovel he had used to clear away the earth around the ladder, he now worked at digging a hole. He chose a spot near the tree that Sam Manila wanted him to cut down. The vulture maintained its distance, but now and then it tested Rusty by trying to get closer. Each time, Rusty picked up the machete and threatened it away.

With the thickness of the weeds and shrubbery, he struggled to make progress on the hole. Finally, he used the machete to clear some of the foliage away.

His work revealed ladder rungs sticking up out of the earth.

There, where he lived.

He dropped the machete and stared.

Sensing a change in Rusty's attitude, the vulture grew bolder and came close enough to the panther's body to begin tearing away at its flesh.

Rusty didn't care anymore.

What had the voice said earlier?

Are you the new occupant?

Beneath his feet, something new waited to take over. A new occupant lying in a kind of slumber, nurtured by the tree's root system, its form and body shaped from the vomit of worms. This new occupant would dress like all the others and look like all the others and wave to all the others as it wasted the groundwater by spraying it all over the brand-new driveway that would appear overnight, once they moved Rusty out. It would use automatic weapons to shoot befuddled wildlife that wandered onto the property.

Or maybe it held an occupant a long, long time ago, and Rusty simply couldn't remember. But that seemed impossible, and so Rusty dismissed that thought.

But still, nothing seemed clear anymore.

Except that nature would defend itself any way that it could, even by becoming the very thing that threatened it.

But not if Rusty could stop it.

He continued to clear away the brush that grew around the ladder. Just as he reached the hatch, he heard sirens and the sound of police cars pulling up outside.

This made him act with haste.

He didn't know if those running in his direction came from the same place as Sam Manila and his family, or if they would meet him with violence. He didn't pause to consider if whatever grew in the nursery below would begin its climb and reach him first. He didn't even consider if its occupant had already emerged and taken its place in a house like his own, perhaps so long ago it had forgotten where it came from.

But he would soon find out.

With machete in hand, he began his descent.

RED MOON LODGE
S.R. Miller

"**O**w, shit!**"** Devin's voice rose beneath the towering trees, high and reedy with pain. He went to one knee on the rough trail, nearly dragging Lynn down with him. "Hold on, I can't—"

"Babe, are you okay?" Lynn asked, her voice equal parts concern and exasperation. It hadn't been long at all since Devin had fallen and hurt his leg, but he'd already taken to hamming up the injury. Lynn, as his girlfriend, had naturally been expected to devote her attention to this, but she was a sensible woman, and her tolerance was wearing thin.

Marcus turned from his position at the head of their little procession, adjusting the straps of the heavy pack upon his shoulders. He'd tried to be diplomatic about the matter, but they had more pressing concerns than Devin's increasingly low tolerance for pain.

"We have to keep moving," Marcus said.

"Yeah?" Devin said, a sneer on his narrow face as he lifted his head to regard Marcus. "Well, why don't you go on ahead then? Let me know how that works out for you."

"The others—" Marcus began, but Devin didn't let him finish.

"Oh, hang the others!" he said. "They shouldn't have gone off on their own in the first place." He winced as he again tried to put weight on his leg. "Fucking thing. I think it's twisted."

Devin was short and lean with a temperament to match. There was sweat on his brow despite the pleasant mountain air, standing out like glittering beads beneath his dark hair. There was a bandage wrapped around his left leg, occupying the space between the hem of his shorts and the top of one sock, though the wound was little more than a bad scrape—at least on the surface.

Marcus cared little for the man, considering him juvenile and aggressive. But he tolerated him, for Lynn's sake, and had done a good enough job of it too, he thought. The trip was wearing on his nerves—*Devin* was wearing on his nerves—and the abrupt and unexplained absence of the others only made things worse.

There had been five of them when they'd set out from Portland, bound for a multi-day backpacking trek through the Cascades. Summers were getting hotter in the valley, and the cool mountain air had been a welcome prospect. Danny and Kyle were experienced hikers and campers, and had been happy to put together the itinerary, and happier still to get back to doing what they loved in the great outdoors. Despite the fact that he—as well as Lynn and Devin—had been invited along for the trip, Marcus had gotten the impression more than once that their addition to the group was not welcome. And so it was perhaps not as shocking as it could have been when Marcus awoke that morning to find Danny and Kyle gone, gear and all.

Marcus left Devin to take yet another break they couldn't afford, shrugging out of his own heavy pack and moving a ways up the inclined trail. The trees towered overhead, the canopy high, the underbrush an almost otherworldly place, green and impossibly verdant. It was beautiful—crisp, clean and still—but circumstance had soured the view in Marcus's eyes.

Lynn left Devin to sit on a fallen log, leaving her pack behind and following Marcus a ways up the trail. The sound of Devin's voice came with her, addressing no one in particular.

"Any room for more complaints?" Lynn said when she'd arrived next to Marcus. "I'm sure you're tired of hearing people bitch, but this sunburn is a real pain." She'd rolled up the sleeves of her flannel shirt, and now poked irritably at her vaguely pink forearms. She'd been pale when they set out from the city, her complexion a perfect complement to her red hair, but then she had decided to lay out in the sun the previous day. That hadn't been a wise choice, but Marcus didn't have the heart to tell her; he was rather taken with the view.

"You'd think I'd be used to it by now," she continued, casting a sidelong glance in Marcus's direction and offering him a little smile. "I guess you don't have to worry about that, huh?"

Marcus looked to his own forearms, the skin there as dark as it ever was. He gave Lynn back a little laugh, no more than he thought was expected of him. She didn't mean any harm by it, after all, and Marcus forgave her. He forgave her a lot, in fact—had been doing it for all the years they'd known each other—not that it ever got him anywhere. Lynn was here with Devin, after all.

"You really think they're still out there?" Lynn asked, before realizing the potentially morbid connotations. "I mean, you think we'll catch up to them?"

Marcus cast a glance back to where Devin sat on his log, poking at his bandaged leg. "At the rate we're going? Not a chance."

They'd woken up that morning to find Danny and Kyle gone. No one had heard them leave, but then they wouldn't have, would they? Danny and Kyle preferred to sleep *beneath the stars*, as they called it; apparently they had no need for the tents the others used to keep all this nature at a peaceable distance. So there had been no camp for them to break, no tents to pack—nothing that might have made the kind of noise that would have woken Marcus and the others from their weary slumber. And the fact that they'd apparently made no noise at all led Marcus to the one thing he considered a reliable fact in all this uncertainty: that Danny and Kyle had *wanted* to slip out unnoticed.

"I still don't get it," Lynn said. "Why would they go off on their own?"

Marcus shook his head. "I dunno," he said. "But I keep telling myself they must have wanted to get on ahead. Maybe they thought we were slowing them down, right? Maybe they just wanted a little time to set their own pace, so they went on ahead. I mean, we're all going in the same direction, so we'll catch up to them." He paused, looking once more into all that great, green wilderness. "At least, that's what I thought."

"But they don't know about..." She nudged her head back toward Devin. "And no one's got a damn signal out here, so there's no way to tell them to come back."

"There sure isn't," Marcus agreed. "And there's no telling how far they're gonna get before they stop and think something might be wrong."

Lynn stared off into the distance for a while, her eyes following the rough trail as it wound its way up toward the next ridge—the presence of which was more felt than seen; the trees made it impossible to see much of the world around them. Out here the sun was little more than a golden dapple on the undergrowth, the mountains that defined this expansive wilderness masked behind a veil of green.

"I don't think they'd just leave us here," Lynn said finally, her pale eyes troubled.

"What are you saying?"

"I mean, what if they didn't leave us?" she said. "What if something... I dunno, what if they didn't leave by choice?"

"They packed up before they left," Marcus reminded her. "Their sleeping bags and their backpacks were gone. If something like a... I dunno, like a mountain lion came in and snatched them up, I don't think they would have taken their gear. And I think we'd have heard it."

"Yeah, sure," Lynn said, but she didn't look reassured. "I just don't think they would have left us, Marcus. I just don't."

"Only thing we can do is keep going, alright? We'll keep at it in the same direction and see what we see."

Lynn said nothing, just nodded her head, and that would have to be good enough. Marcus picked up his backpack, shrugging it into place on his tired shoulders.

"Hey, break time's over!" he called back down the trail to where Devin sat. "Let's get at it!"

Devin called something back, the words lost over the distance, though the meaning was clear enough. Lynn sighed and trudged back down the trail to help.

#

The day continued just as it had, and Devin's injury seemed to be getting worse, not better. Whether he was exaggerating or not, the result was the same: Marcus and Lynn had to take turns helping him along where the trail became steep, and the breaks became more frequent. It was on one such break that they first discovered the vines.

"What song is that?" Marcus asked. He'd been fidgeting with his pack where he sat beside the trail, but now turned his attention to Lynn, who was absently adjusting the straps of her backpack for lack of anything better to do.

"What?" she said. "What song?"

"The song you were just humming," Marcus said. "It sounds familiar, but I can't place it. It's driving me nuts."

"I wasn't humming anything."

"You're sure?"

Lynn nodded, and the both of them looked toward Devin, who sat sprawled beside a large rock grumbling to himself. He certainly wasn't humming. Marcus shook his head. Lynn laughed nervously.

"What is it?" she asked.

"I just..." Marcus looked into the darkness of the trees, where dusk had come prematurely. "I swear I heard—"

They all heard it then: a tune that was as directionless as it was maddeningly familiar. A melody that lingered just at the range of their hearing.

"Is that it?" Lynn asked.

Marcus only stared back at her, seeing now that there was no way the sound had come from her after all. Even as she spoke the sound rose and fell beneath the gloomy green canopy, sweet but melancholy.

"It must be someone nearby," Lynn said, peering out into the forest. "Maybe it's Danny and Kyle fucking with us?"

Marcus wanted to believe that, but there was little time to convince himself of this before a sudden exclamation from Devin caught his attention and held it firm.

"Whoa!" he cried out, shuffling sideways in alarm and nearly falling over. "Dude. *Dude!* Look at this shit!"

"What is it?" Lynn asked, looking unsure of whether or not she was supposed to be concerned.

"Check it out," Devin said, struggling to his feet and pointing into the brush behind the rock he'd been leaning against. "It's these vines. Man, I think they were..." He trailed off, shaking his head, apparently doubting his own words. He gave a nervous chuckle, hopping a little as he shifted his weight. "Jesus, I think they were *singing*."

But the sound of that humming voice was gone by the time Marcus and Lynn arrived, peering into the green tangle alongside the trail. And indeed there were vines, just as Devin had said. They were ghostly pale—like the color of the full moon on a cold night, with tufts of fleshy leaves sprouting from the blooms, resembling bellflowers.

"They're just vines," Lynn said.

"Well, that freaky singing was coming from somewhere, wasn't it?" Devin said. "And I swear, it was *right* behind me. You see anything else there?"

"Vines don't sing, man," Marcus said, though his eyes lingered on the vines, on the pale, cold color of the blooms.

"Yeah, well, I know what I heard," Devin said, making another ungainly hop before finally settling himself down on the rock. "And I know vines don't fucking sing, alright? Not *normal* vines. But there's something wrong with this mountain. Maybe no one else is saying it, but we're all thinking it. Danny and Kyle didn't just wander off for the hell of it. There's something—"

"Well, all the more reason to keep moving then, huh?" Marcus turned and began to head back toward where he'd dropped his pack, eager to move on, to catch up to Danny and Kyle—or so he told himself.

"Are you out of your mind?" Devin said. "Look at that trail! There's no way I'm gonna make it up there. Not in this condition. Unless you two are gonna carry me up there, I'm done for the day."

Marcus hated to admit it, but Devin was right. The trail ahead rose steeply toward the next ridge, the way uneven and no doubt treacherous even by the light of day—and what little light they had left was rapidly fading. They had flashlights, sure, and maybe they could make it a little further, but there was no telling how far they would have to climb before they found another spot suitable for setting up camp. Here, at least the ground was relatively even. But up there, there was no telling what they would find—or how badly they might hurt themselves trying to reach it.

"Fine," Marcus said. "But we're starting early tomorrow. We've got a lot of lost time to make up for."

That was true, of course. But what Marcus didn't say—and what all of them surely felt—was that he didn't want to spend a minute longer in this strange, dark place.

The three of them pitched their tents, ate a simple meal, and went to bed early.

#

Marcus woke abruptly in the night, fearing it was the phantom singing that had roused him. But the truth was worse. Lynn was screaming, her voice rising in brittle terror, the sound causing Marcus's heart to hammer in his chest.

He grabbed his flashlight and scrambled out of his tent, tripping as he emerged into the cold night air. He went down on his hands and knees but kept moving anyway, hurling himself through the dark toward Lynn's tent.

"Lynn!" Marcus called, reaching the tent. "Lynn, what is it? What's wrong?" He opened the tent zipper with trembling hands.

And then he saw the vines.

They had gotten inside the tent somehow, working their way through the base of the door to where Devin lay sleeping, his feet toward the tent flap. But he wasn't sleeping now: his eyes were wide, his mouth open in an almost comical expression of shock. His lips moved, forming words that no one heard, his voice lost somewhere in his throat. His hands clawed uselessly at his shorts while he stared down at his injured leg—at the bandages that were placed there to cover his wounds. Those bandages were now blotchy with fresh blood.

"The vines!" Lynn cried. "Marcus, the vines, they're..."

She didn't need to tell him what was happening. Marcus could see well enough that the vines had come for Devin, pushing beneath the edge of his bandages to get at the wound beneath. Seeing this, *knowing* what was happening, did nothing to lessen the shock of what he saw, nor could it explain how it was possible. Plants just didn't do that—did they?

"Okay, hold on," Marcus said, temporarily stunned by what he'd stumbled into, yet forcing himself to act. "We'll just get rid of these..."

He grabbed hold of the offending vines and began to pull, drawing an immediate scream from Devin. Marcus let go at once, and not just because of Devin's reaction; when he pulled on the vine, he'd felt it *move.*

"It's in me," Devin gasped. His chest fluttered as he struggled to breathe. "I can feel it *moving.* God, it's in my fucking leg!"

Marcus turned to Lynn. "Where's his knife?"

"What?"

"Knife, dammit!" he said. "We need to cut the bandage and get these... these *whatever* the fuck they are out of here! Where's Devin's knife?"

Lynn understood and frantically began to paw through the clutter of clothes and supplies in the small tent, eventually coming back with a small folding knife. She handed it over, and Marcus flipped it open.

"I need you to hold him still," he said, nudging his head toward Devin. "If he starts moving around, I might cut him."

Lynn nodded and positioned herself so her hands were on Devin's leg. Though how necessary all that was, who could say; Devin had collapsed back onto his sleeping bag.

Marcus took hold of the edge of the bandage, worked the point of the knife beneath it, and cut it away as carefully as he could. When he saw what was beneath it, he felt his own breath leave him in a rush.

Devin was right: the vines hadn't just wrapped around his wounded leg—they had crawled *inside* of it. Fresh blood welled up from the wounds and now began to run freely.

"Oh my god," Lynn said, her voice low and desperate. "Oh my god, oh my god, oh my god..."

"Quiet," Marcus said, again nudging his head toward Devin. "We can't have him panicking, and if you panic then he will, and then I will, and then..."

"Alright," Lynn said, taking a deep breath. "Okay, sure. Keep it together."

"First thing's first," Marcus said as he reached out and again took hold of the cluster of vines that had pushed into Devin's leg. Devin made a low, nauseous sound, but he lacked the strength to offer much

42

protest now. Emboldened and wanting it to be over with, Marcus pulled at the vines, feeling his stomach turn over as he watched the thin, wiry tips withdraw from the raw wound. He'd brought out no more than half an inch before a coiled length of vine wrapped around Devin's ankle; it cinched tightly—and then pulled.

Devin was jerked toward the tent door. Marcus grabbed hold of him, pressing him down into the sleeping bag as the vines pulled harder, trying to drag him out into the dark.

"Hold him!" Marcus cried, trying to keep a grip on Devin and fumble with the knife at the same time. Lynn was shocked but did what she was told, grabbing hold of Devin beneath the arms as the vines gave another savage jerk.

Marcus took hold of the bundle of vines—they were waxy to the touch and trembled with an impossible, wiry strength—and then he brought down the knife as hard as he could.

Tense as they were, the vines cut free with a dramatic flail, jerking out of the tent and thrashing in the undergrowth. Those that were left behind in Devin's leg moved like green worms, wriggling with no clear direction or purpose. Before he could lose his nerve, Marcus reached out and yanked them free of Devin's leg, then tossed the bloody tendrils out of the tent.

In the trees outside a sound rose—a melody both sweet and melancholy, drifting in the dark. It was joined by the sound of the vines, thrashing through the undergrowth as they withdrew into the forest. There was another sound as well, a familiar sound that, like the music, came from everywhere and nowhere.

It sounded like laughter.

#

No sooner than Devin was patched up and bandaged, Marcus began to break camp, eager to move. Day would be coming soon, and he was in no mood to sit around and wait. The strange, singing voice had quieted, but everyone had seen enough to be afraid. They knew something was out there.

Devin was in shock, but once it began to abate, the fear of what lurked in the trees gave him a motivation he'd not possessed the day before, and he was on his feet despite his injury. He moved a little slower than Marcus and Lynn as they hurriedly took down their tents and readied their packs, but he was every bit as eager to get moving. To get away.

Dawn came, and they were nearly ready to hit the trail when Lynn stopped abruptly and turned her eyes toward the trail leading up the mountain.

"Who's there?" Lynn asked, alarm obvious in her voice. No one was in the mood for surprises.

"What?" Marcus said, turning from where he'd been busy stowing the last of his gear. Devin, too, turned to look, careful to give the edge of the undergrowth a wide berth.

"There's someone..." Lynn said, taking a step back from where the trail disappeared into the darkness beneath the trees. She pointed. "Look, right there. There's someone on the trail."

"Hello?" Marcus called, raising his voice and hoping it would be mistaken for confidence. To his own ears his voice was too thin, too uncertain. "Can we help you?"

Devin, past the point of caring about what anyone might think, turned on his flashlight and shined it into the dark mouth of the trail. Eyes stared back at him from a stoic face, as there was indeed someone standing there—a man with a rather curious appearance.

He was dressed strangely, his features and hair suggesting he might have been Native American. But his dress was like nothing Marcus could identify, modern or traditional, and indeed he would have been hard pressed even to describe it if he'd had to. Something about the man lent him an alien quality, an impression that was not helped in the least by the unsettling stare he leveled upon each of them. His eyes were oddly empty of emotion, regarding the group with no more than casual interest.

"Hey man," Devin said. "What the fuck are you doing out there?" The man carried no supplies, had nothing at all but his strange clothes.

Marcus stepped forward, drawing closer to Lynn, who had begun to move back toward the center of their little clearing. The man gave no answer to Devin's question.

"The others," Marcus said. "Have you seen them on the trail ahead? You came from that way, didn't you? You must have seen them—two men, about my age."

For a time it seemed the man would only go on staring, ignoring the question just as he'd done before. But at last he spoke, and like his clothes, his voice was like nothing Marcus had heard before—different not because of any accent he could identify, but for its very sound.

"There were others," the man confirmed. "Yes, not long ago. They will have reached the lodge by now."

"Lodge?" Lynn said, confused—and then hopeful. "Wait, there's a lodge up here?"

"The Red Moon Lodge," the man answered. "You will find it at the top of the ridge."

"Yeah, sure," Devin said. "Whatever, man. They got phones up there? My leg's busted up, and I am *not* going all the way back down this fucking mountain."

"You will find what you seek there," the man said. "And you'll find the others as well."

"Good enough for me," Devin said, shining his flashlight on his pack and the rest of his gear. "I'm ready to get the hell off this mountain."

"Wait," Marcus said, speaking to the man he could no longer see. Without the flashlight, the darkness had rushed in to fill the space where he stood, plunging the trail into shadow. "I don't know if we'll make it that far, not with his leg and..." He couldn't bring himself to mention what they'd seen in the night, what had happened with the vines. "Is there any way you can have them send help down for us? Like a ranger or something? Shit, even if you could tell Danny and Kyle to come back and help. Anything."

"Yeah," Lynn said, sounding hopeful. "I mean, you came from there, right? You don't have any gear, and... yeah, you *must* have just come from there. Is that it?"

The man didn't respond.

"Sir?" Lynn called into the trees, what little hope she'd had gone from her voice now. "Sir, are you there?"

"Look man, I'll pay you," Marcus said. He hadn't liked the arrival of the man, and his presence put him on edge, but the sudden silence was worse. "We'll work something out, alright?" When there was again no response, Marcus pulled his own flashlight from his pack and clicked it on, shining it into the darkness at the mouth of the trail.

The man was gone.

"Hey, wait!" Lynn called, jogging ahead to where the clearing met the trail.

"Lynn!" Marcus called, hurrying after her and catching her with a hand upon her shoulder.

"Where the hell did he go?" she asked, her eyes searching the way forward. The trail rose, rocky and uneven toward the ridge, the way forward as obvious as it was perilous. But there was no sign of the man there.

"Spooky," Devin said.

"Maybe he's got his own trail," Marcus said. "He's clearly familiar with the area."

"That's one way of putting it," Devin said scornfully. "Fucking weirdo probably lives out here."

"But there's a lodge," Lynn said.

"Is there?" Devin said doubtfully. "Danny and Kyle had us going over the map how many times? And they never mentioned anything about a lodge, or whatever. I thought their whole point in coming this way was to *avoid* people."

"Maybe they just missed it," Lynn said. "And anyway, that guy said Danny and Kyle were already there, didn't he? So we can meet up with them, and then we can figure out what to do from there."

Marcus sighed. "Devin?"

"What? You're concerned about what I think all of a sudden?" Devin said, looking thoughtful nonetheless. "Well, we can't go all the way back down—that would take *days*. So if this lodge is just up the trail, then I say we go there."

Lynn nodded, then looked to Marcus. But Marcus didn't want to make that call, didn't want to agree with them. Because the truth was...

there was something about the man and what he'd said that wasn't sitting right with him. The others surely caught that, just as he did—caught it, and still agreed to carry on, because there really wasn't much choice. Devin was right: going back down the way they'd come would take days, even if no one was injured. And that was a lot of time to be out there, especially now that they knew what lurked in the undergrowth.

Lodge or no lodge, they would continue on course.

#

The day passed much like the previous one, with Lynn and Marcus taking turns helping Devin along the difficult terrain. But to be fair, Devin did what he could, more motivated now that he knew what was at stake. The vines were still out there, after all; on more than one occasion the party had seen them coiled in the undergrowth along the trail, their pale flowers bobbing in the breeze. Occasionally snatches of that strange melody would carry out of the trees, ensuring no one forgot where they were going—or why.

There was no sign of the lodge they sought, even as they finally reached level ground atop the ridge. There was, however, proof of what they all feared: they would be spending another night out in the wild. The sun was setting, and with no clear destination in sight, there was no choice but to set up camp and wait until morning to continue the search.

They scouted a bit of level ground where the trees had grown sparse and where, more importantly, there was no sign of the vines. There they made camp and settled in for the night.

#

Hours passed with Marcus in his tent, unable to sleep. His ears were trained to the dark world just outside, clinging to every little sound as if something sinister might be approaching. Twice he'd gotten up with his flashlight and made a circuit of their camp, checking the underbrush for any sign of the vines, or the strange man they'd met that morning. But there was no sign of either, and he'd been forced to return to his tent. Still, sleep would not come.

Tomorrow, he told himself. *I'll sleep tomorrow.* They'd find the lodge, and there they'd be safe. Danny and Kyle would be there, and all their questions would be answered. Marcus could finally relax and get the sleep he so desperately craved.

He was nearly ready to get up once more and make another check of the camp when he heard something—not in the woods outside, but in his own tent. This was no stealthy movement, no whisper of fibrous vines on nylon. No, this was an ordinary sound, but one wholly unexpected: the low, humming pulse of his cellphone vibrating.

Marcus reached into the side pocket of his pack and pulled out his phone, wondering if maybe he'd picked up a signal at last. The phone said otherwise, spelled out in the status bar at the top of the screen. Curiously though, Marcus had a text message. And not from just anyone—but from Lynn.

Marcus opened the message; it was a picture. Even as he looked at it, he saw that his phone was loading another incoming message, and more after that one.

The first photo was a selfie, a pretty standard shot of Lynn's face— the sort he'd seen plenty of times before, the angle just right. She looked gorgeous even with the sunburn. But there were more pictures, many more, and his phone loaded the next image in the sequence. His breath came in with a sharp gasp, and he held it.

She was topless, the high angle of the camera looking down over the peaks of her breasts and the long valley that led to the waist of her pants. Her skin was ghostly pale, washed out by the flash of her camera; only the faint, pink tinge of her sunburned arm and the rosy nubs of her nipples were colored. Though it was hard to tell for sure, Marcus thought she was lying on her back in the grass—a possibility that at once excited him, but also filled him with dread.

The next image loaded, and all thoughts went quiet, all attention diverted to what Marcus saw on his screen. The image was like the first, only now her pants had gone the way of her shirt, and there was nothing beneath them, nothing at all. He could see her white legs, posed coyly as if she were on a beach somewhere, as if that might have been the sea just past her and not an ocean of dark, treacherous trees.

The final message loaded, not a picture this time, but simple text: "Come outside."

Marcus crept from his tent, unsure of what he was doing, unsure of *everything,* knowing only that he'd wanted this—yes, even *hoped* for it, on this very trip—and now it was happening. He carried his flashlight with him but did not turn it on, afraid to wake Devin. He wouldn't need it, anyway; the moon had risen—a great, bleached-bone face in the sky that shed its chilly light on the entire camp.

"Lynn?" Marcus called, as quietly as he could. There was a sound from the edge of camp, a rustling of leaves. "Lynn, where are you?"

"Over here," she said, her voice quiet, committed to the secrecy of their rendezvous. Marcus bumbled his way past the trees that grew closest to camp, picking his way through the undergrowth. Lynn giggled. "Almost there," she said.

And there she was, pale and exquisite in a shaft of moonlight. The light did delightful things to her skin, turned her hair to brushed copper. Marcus's eyes saw it all at once, drinking her in as his legs carried him unsteadily toward her. There was a little clearing at the base of the tree, a soft carpet of dried pine needles beneath her bare feet that matched the color of her hair.

"What is this?" Marcus asked stupidly, hating to but needing to say something.

Lynn smiled, her pale eyes lighting in the gloom. "What you want," she answered. "You deserve it, don't you think? After everything?"

He did, of course. Something in the back of his brain had told him as much all along, insisted that *he* was the one that deserved her, as he'd watched her bound from one failed relationship to the next, entangling herself with one asshole or another. *Yes,* that voice told him. Now it was *his* time.

Lynn silenced his dumb, questioning lips with her own, drawing him in with arms that closed tightly around him. And then she moved lower, her copper hair catching the moonlight as she sank to her knees, her deft fingers working at his belt, and then his pants. He turned his eyes upward to the moon that glared down at him like a leering skull.

Lynn closed around him, enveloped him. The wind sighed in the undergrowth, and Lynn, practiced, efficient—eagerly drew him in, ever tighter.

"Marcus?" a voice called. "What are you doing out there?"

Marcus turned his eyes toward that voice, where he saw Lynn in the dead bone light of the moon—not naked and yearning, but dressed just as she had been, weary and concerned. She fumbled with her flashlight, but even before she'd managed to turn it on and shine it into the trees, Marcus turned his eyes to the ground at his feet—to the dark mass that had closed in around him.

The vines tittered, voices like children, amused by some great game. Marcus screamed, his hands flailing, swatting and tearing at the thick, sinuous growths that had wound around his legs and waist. Flowers bobbed in the moonlight like laughing faces, leaves twisting like greedy hands.

Lynn came down the shallow decline, her light preceding her and illuminating the horror there. Marcus thrashed, Lynn pulled, smacking and kicking at the vines that closed in around them. Somehow Marcus managed to get free, but still he screamed as he and Lynn struggled back into camp together, the voices of the vines raised in amusement at their backs.

"We have to go!" Lynn yelled. "We have to get out of here!"

Marcus couldn't find the words, but the wild look in his eyes must have been agreement enough, because Lynn turned and hurried back toward her tent.

Marcus pulled his phone from his pocket, opening his messages, already knowing what he would see there: nothing. There were no texts from Lynn, no pictures. He'd imagined all of it. Somehow the vines had gotten into his head just as surely as they'd gotten into Devin's wounds the day before. And if Lynn hadn't come out of her tent to find him out there in the dark...

"Devin!" Lynn called as she reached the tent. "Devin, get up! We have to—" And then it was her turn to scream.

Marcus hurried toward the tent, toward the piercing sound of

Lynn's voice, and together they watched as Devin was dragged from the tent. Vines entwined around him in a fleshy, green tangle, but there were no screams from Devin, no struggle as he was pulled into the woods.

Lynn rushed forward to help, but Marcus grabbed her by the arm and dragged her back. The treeline issued a low, sinister *hiss,* a sound that rose to accompany the sound of the laughing, twisting vines. The sounds came from everywhere at once, rising in the night air as if the forest itself was alive.

"Come on," Marcus urged, tugging on Lynn's arm and forcibly turning her away from the bloody tent.

Lynn went with him, grudgingly at first, and then more willingly as the vine's reaching fingers once more emerged from the darkness of the treeline, eager to claim another body. They went together then, Lynn and Marcus, leaving their little camp behind, running through the dark as fast as their legs would carry them.

#

The forest withdrew and the ground became stony and sharp as they reached the highest ridge. There, the moon revealed all with its stark, cold light. But there was no lodge here, and surely they'd have seen it if there was: a building in the distance, lights in its windows, a welcoming sight in this barren, gray hell, so bleak after days beneath the lush trees of the lower slopes. Here the trees were sparse, stunted things, whose skeletal branches reached toward the night sky like grasping fingers, catching the light.

Still they ran, Marcus and Lynn, stumbling, falling, yet always regaining their feet and pressing on, thinking little of where they were now—only what was behind them, and what had been promised up ahead. And they found it, just as they'd been told they would. They stopped at once as the lodge finally revealed itself to them.

On the ground before them was a depression—a perfect circle perhaps twenty feet across and a foot deep. Stones lined its outer perimeter, and just outside of these, growing from points around the circle, were strange trees, twisted in the moonlight.

There was no building, no phones, no help—nothing they'd come to expect. There was only this place, this grim circle that served to gather the light of the moon as it passed above the ridge.

Marcus stepped toward one of the trees at the circle's edge, realizing it wasn't a tree after all. The vines were everywhere, growing in a rich, vertical tangle, their blooms bobbing in the night air like small, grinning faces. But there was more, of course. There was something within those vines, something the vines had climbed upon and woven through to form these structures. Lynn realized the truth, even as Marcus saw what was just before his eyes. Her voice rose in a scream that carried down the mountain.

"Oh my god," Lynn gasped. "Devin, oh my god, oh my—"

She grabbed at the vines that bound Devin, that held his face craned toward the sky, his arms outstretched as if to draw the moon down upon him. The vines hissed as her fingers found them, and Lynn stepped back with a strangled cry, collapsing onto the stony ground.

Marcus walked about the circle, looking at each pillar in turn. Just as he expected, he found Kyle and Danny—both with milky eyes gazing up to the heavens. There were others, of course—bodies Marcus did not recognize, some old, some seemingly ancient, each of them host to these strange, murderous vines, each of them twisted into the shape of a tree, staring into the sky.

Marcus was speechless; it was all he could do just to breathe.

"He's alive," Lynn said, her voice small but desperate. "Marcus, it's Devin. He's... look, he's still alive!"

And he must have been, for Marcus heard a low, croaking sound, as if someone were struggling to speak with a dry throat. But as he began to move toward Lynn and Devin, he realized the sound had not come from there, but from beside him. Marcus followed the sound, turning his eyes upward toward the dried, mummified face of one of those old, dead things within the vines. Its mouth was moving, and from its dried lips came a sound that was not speech—but song.

Marcus stumbled backward, nearly falling into the circular depression. The sound rose all around him, issuing from dead lips, corpses old and new alike. Danny, Kyle, and even Devin joined in, their voices rising toward the night sky, thin and strained but managing a familiar melody all the same. This was the song they'd heard the day before—the song Devin insisted the vines had been singing.

The light that tinted those upturned faces began to change, becoming pink, and then a bright, vivid red. Marcus and Lynn turned their faces upward, gazing into the night sky just as the others gathered around the circle. And there was the moon, huge, impossible, its skull face no longer the color of bone, but the color of blood. It bore down upon them as if it meant to crush them, this massive, red face in the sky. Voices rose to honor it, corpses and vines, open mouths and bobbing bellflowers, all issuing their melody to that great, red behemoth, drawing it down to meet them.

Marcus and Lynn raised their voices as well, their screams echoing across the mountain, their voices breaking with their minds as they beheld that which awaited them. Soon, they sang as well, new voices for the red god, new voices for the coiled growths which had brought them here to bear witness to this—a place of worship.

Marcus realized he could no longer look down. The moon held his eyes transfixed, and his neck would not move. He could not see the ground beneath him or the others around him. But if he had looked down, he knew what he would see: the vines coiled about his body, growing around him, growing into him, rooting him to this holy place and making him a part of it.

He could not remember how he'd come here, or why. Such thoughts were trivial, useless now that his potential had been realized. All thoughts of who he was and who he might have been now faded in the red light, elevating him even as it rooted him within the lodge.

The light burned his eyes, and Marcus welcomed it. He opened his mouth, and once more began to sing.

GIANT KILLER
Amelia Gorman

Call me Paul the evergrowing, Paul the unslowing glacier of a man who has been known to scrape his forehead on the stars. Paul who must but whisper, and it rustles the dusty fields of Mars, Neptune, Pluto, and beyond. Have you ever licked the aurora and had it frozen for a second on your tongue? I have.

I grew up on the plains of Minnesota, and up and up and up some more. Until the plains of Minnesota receded like a distant shore. Birches turned to twigs while my bones competed with each other—the clouds slowly smothered the ground. Still I got taller and taller every day, pissing new rivers into being.

This could all be hyperbole. Maybe I was seven, maybe ten feet tall. But all growth is a kind of horror as yourself expands inside you. It's hard enough to watch where a dozen of your past selves died, marked and notched on a wooden door—that's the kind of growth a family can handle. No door was built to hold a man like me, as I burst older out of the child I once was.

Imagine the thickest boil you can, swelling with the richest gout. Imagine bones creaking and shouting, skin shrieking in a protest of growth. I downed a cow every morning and still mowed grass with my jaws, demanding every slim calorie within my reach.

I grew up in Minnesota, until Minnesota grew too small for me. What followed was a heavy tread to the west, hollowing new lakes in my footprints where you might ice fish next winter and think of me. I rode a monstrous sawhorse across the Great Plains to where a bigger horizon lay. And I grew taller every day. And taller and taller. I dragged nothing but a bindle and my ax in my wake, plowing furrows and digging canyons in the narrow valleys.

To see the ocean cresting over the ridge was to behold a home. I followed my ears to the roar of the surf. To see that big blue drink that can never run out filled my giant heart, and it still had more to give. I walked high on the dry Sierras, soaking up the nearness of the sun, the coolness of the clouds. I brushed my hands against the fringed tops of the sequoias, and let them tickle my palms. Yes, to come to the ocean was to come home.

I bathed my tired muscles in Thor's sinkhole, where leviathans frolic under the swollen waves. You've never seen huge until you've watched the slick things that only live where there is no air to weigh them down. I befriended a young calf of a blue whale, named her Kind, and we chased eels and stranger things that lie under the foam.

But I still grew lonely, because all I do is grow. And what is a home without a family? I wasn't complete until I stumbled on the loggers, hauling their skid camp through fields of lumber. They weren't horrified—they were delighted of me. They found me a canvas tent as big as a field, and I built bridges over rivers to the sea. We boiled cauldrons of soup and roasted whole elk on spits.

This was it; this was all I needed.

#

My name is Jack, Jack the Giant Killer, from a long line of giant killers. They stood strong on each others' shoulders to topple even the tallest tyrants. They hacked at wide ankles with axes, shouting "Timber!" all the while. They staked down feet and knifed tendons while tenderly raising a generation to take on the job after. That's me. A family tree painted on the parlor wall ties us back to the killers of Gogmagog and Blunderbore. We seeded ourselves all over the world, both old and new, and grew like angry thistles, wild and willful for blood.

Like my mother, who killed giants so fast she ran into herself getting up as she was coming home to bed. Margit the Giant Killer (although I called her ma) was the hero who poisoned the bay, bringing death to Bres and Brammert. She harvested hemlock for weeks before she had enough to fill that basin. Fish wouldn't swim there for years, and vultures feasted for decades. Children can swim there now. And in the meantime my mother killed. And killed and killed. She killed Korb and Brant, and she killed the Hurdy Gurdy Family that flattened villages. Children live there now.

Ma raised me in a creaky little house. Or more to the point, I raised myself as she was so often gone a-killing that even her bedbugs starved. I'm short in stature, but I'll be short with you, *I've got no time unless it's time for killing.* That's what her pocket watch says, the one she gave me before she set out on her last adventure.

You know the heap where the poppies make a trail in the meadow? That's my pit trap, and the rotten bodies of Deinos and Dipros are what make the flowers bloom. I'm thinking of growing beans there. I'm going to live up to Ma's reputation if it kills me. And you know it will, because it always does, us Giant-Killers.

I've heard of you, Paul. I saw my future laid out black and white in the newspapers, in the West Coast Signal and the Humboldt Times. *Tall Order as Lumber Camp Titan Rushes to Meet Demands.* Forget the titan... all giants are horrors, even if they don't know it yet. When the famine comes, and a famine is a-coming...

I'm going to kill you, Paul.

So here am I, Jack-of-the-Woods. Jack of the wet wood, the waterlogged stumps, the damp dew. Jack-of-the-working-world. I hide in the branches where a woodpecker pecks like a pile driver. The sun's in my eyes, seizing me in its hot grip. I pull back on my crossbow—the one from my uncle's uncle's mother. Huge limbs are in my sight, like a tiger among the trunks. Your stripes are your skin, presented before me on a platter of hunt.

And crashing through the canopy goes you, Paul, goes you. You goddamn bull. These are living things, precious as bone china in a tea palace in France. While I scamper up my tree like a nimble squirrel, you lumber without a care. You leave waste in your squashing tracks—here a beaver dam, there a bee hive.

When I was a baby boy, I put a nail in a tree. The tree didn't do so well, Paul. It stopped growing, grayed and died. Copper is a killer, so I shoot you full of spikes, Paul. You monster, you're nimble for the gross

57

thing you are, but you're still nailed by my copper shot. Girdled and gaping, you'll be thirsty and hungry forever more.

Your blood pitter patters like rain, giving new meaning to the words *redwood curtain*. Your blood is like piss, like peril that drumbeats your heart. I stalk in the shadows of your spoor. I'm Jack-of-the Footprint. Pitcher plants gape from where you walk, where you run through the woods. I'm snapped at by some flytrap plant—a sundew plant I think—but I'm too quick for them. When there's no more blood they'll thirst for the sun, but there's no sun here in the black black woods.

Your trail leads to the beach, but the spring tides erase your tracks from the sand. There's only a flat level plain where sea stacks tower in the distance like further giants. I hear they're trolls turned to stone by the sun. I can only hope the same for you and your corpse.

#

Sure I run, Jack. Who wouldn't? You would too if you were bleeding from a dozen train spikes in your thighs. You would too if your skin risked sloughing off in sheets like the aurora—the skin under the skin too thin. I have a wicked thirst Jack, because of what you did to me. I grow pale as the moon.

But I've known better killers than you, across this green waste, across the blue, across the geysers and the peaks. There was a sick man, Spring-Heeled-Jack, who could have been your mother's father. He thought he could leap buildings, but it turns out men the size of buildings reaped him. You're no Spring-Heeled-Jack, Jack, and what you don't know about redwoods could fill the ocean.

I lead you across a field of green, because I know my yuletide allies lurk beneath. Frilled and verdant, with scarlet mouths and too many teeth. As they eat the flies and ants, so too are you like an insect to me. Your stings hurt—even make me ill—but in the end they are so small. Pointless are your points. And you cannot run fast through my garden of oversized flytrap and pitcher plants, not if you want your feet intact.

I run to the sea, and she welcomes me with open arms. I bleed as

I meet her embrace. I think I am the oldest son of Sempervirens and Pacific when they loved long ago. Her medicine does not suffice, and the brine stings my throbbing legs. They'll carry me no further, and I know you're somewhere close behind.

Too weak to continue, a familiar wake appears in front of me. It's a road to an island, one I'm too injured to take. The road is followed by its own chariot as Kind breaches the surface and invites me onto her rubbery back. My old friend, now fully grown, smells like krill and salvation. You won't kill me today, Jack.

Behind me, I hear your copper harpoon whistle as the moon rises malevolently above us. I hold Kind's tail tight, and the last arrow goes straight through her marrow. There's blood in the water, sharks chasing us. The fog closes behind us like a gate, and that's your last shot.

We take the wave road to the island, just a sea stack covered in grasses and buckthorn. Sharks and killer whales behind us await their meal. The world is full of killers singing their songs. But I make it, we make it, and Kind makes one last call. Sloughs her body with me up on the beach.

I ate her Jack, and I wept the whole time. I pulled the copper spikes from my legs, tourniqueted them with vines. Some day someone will find them and think there was a railroad here, or great supports stuck into the sea. I can't be killed by copper, and copper can't kill a tree. What you don't know about redwoods Jack, could fill the ocean.

#

I'm Jack, Jack-the-Firestarter, and I inflame hearts all over the coast. Hearts and heartwoods and above all... hard-chested bastards like you, Paul. I'll make you into matches and then I'll burn you up. I could light a fire in a crab basket. I could send a burning wave downhill on a windless day. I could set the seas aflame from here to Hungary if I tried.

And if I can't kill you with nails, Paul, I'll kill you with fire.

I see you every sundown dipping into the whiskey. I see you and your loggers wet your tongues like a sloppy gang on the wagon. I see you tip a barrel back while your partners in lumber use teeny tiny shot glasses. Do you stay with them to feel more a man, Paul? How many trees died to make your mug, you murderer? How many trees died to get you slobbery drunk on huckleberry moonshine?

This is your Friday tradition, I see now. After all the train cars have traversed south to the cities. After you eat your fish cooked on giant skewers. But I know you eat whales to satisfy your endless hunger, pierced barbecue on an alder tree.

And you sing songs, the crowd of you, you sing songs that blow like the breeze. Your breath catches me swinging from branch to branch and nearly knocks me on the ground. But I grab a vine on my way down and shimmy back up that horse, like Ma used to tell me to. I besiege those tower tall trees.

And in my hand, a match for every finger, five red-headed friends. I told you I was good at stealing hearts. I told you I was good at making matches. A family of little mischief makers is ready to burn at my command.

It's been a dry year, and all drought is horror. Tumbleweeds packed up their bags and left their children by the side of the road. Duff goes up with the smallest spark and burns the longest.

They say it's not the heat that gets to you, but I don't care what gets you, Paul, as long as it does.

#

I awake and I rise to the odor of smoke layered over the sound of choking. It smells like bacon, like a sweet young whistle punk has taken it on himself to make a breakfast, a thought, a gift to his peers, but some unclean searing smell beneath it nears and I, I remember a time...

A time when a heat wave stewed some mussels in their husks. Oysters popped open from the heat to give me their pearls. The whole beach was a shellfish boil, a crayfish riot, a party, a sauna, a hell.

And the railway car tonight is its own cooking pot. Call it a brazen bull, a sacrificial craze of murder and suffering. Those tough men do their best not to cry out, but in the end, death always brings out the worst in us.

Foolscap, we called the chef, because he wore the most tatterdemalion tricorn cap, he lay outside the cookwagon in the skid camp. And his skin was burned way back from his face. And his skull emerged like a pearl to the world.

But my skin holds water like a sponge, and I don't feel the heat. I feel the same as a normal sized man but spread out amongst so much more skin, I think. I work through weather, and I weather the unpleasant rays of the sun. I pack them in to save for later. I convert, because up here the air is cleaner. I stomp, slathering the fires out as best I can. But it's too late for everyone, save me.

Take water to cool and calm, it rushes back in. The ocean, my mother, never-ending. Pacific, but I'm anything but peaceful. What you don't know about redwoods Jack, could fill the ocean.

Call me Paul the dying, contrary to what I said before. Call me grieved and grieving. Each time before I swore I wasn't going to stand for this, but this time I will, Jack. Take your ax to me—I give up, I give in. This world is too sick for me, and too small. All I wanted was to grow unburdened like a tree. Will I make a sound when the ax begins to chip away at what's left of me?

The blade goes in my leg, pulls out, and a spray of chunks go with it. I'm Paul, but I'm less and less Paul with every chop and every pull. The air around me more me than my own self. The redwood curtain closes one final time on this, our last performance. I take a final bow, and then timber, I fall one last time. I water the earth like I'm drunk one last time on one final barrel of wine.

If I'm lucky, I imagine I'll see my friends again at the end of all things. Vance noodling out a song on an out-of-tune harmonica, not choking on smoke in a collapsing tent. Or bent on the ground trying to vomit, but there's no more water left in him. Or Merry in his canoe cutting a line in the fog.

All loss is horror, but it's pacification too. I hope my body responds like a whalefall, cooking a primordial stew, eaten by mushrooms as much as I ate fruit from those big shelves. I can feel their tendrils reaching for me now. I hope for its sake it doesn't grow too much.

My vision grows dark. There is no more aurora for me.

#

All the roles I've been, all the roles I'll ever be—they all flash before my eyes, even as you're the one dying. Call me Lumber-Jack, woodsman and hewer. I've been sharpening my ax on diamonds, Paul. I heard it whistle on the wheel until the edge could slice a strand of hair. It can cut a mote of dust, or a sunbeam.

I don't know why you won't run away. Where's the fight, the feud I grew to love? Where's the Paul who pushes back against me, who runs through wild rivers and cruel gardens to get away? You were almost like family, such a constant in my life.

And instead, now I lop you down like a sequoia. You fall and the earth quakes. Buildings by the bay are toppling. Roofs cave, and caves are filling with fallen stalactites. There'll be a new lake where your head landed on the soil.

But one less giant is one less giant, and I'm satisfied, if underwhelmed. My body still trembles from the quake. My arms vibrate until the ax shaft snaps in two. I wash your blood off of me in the Pacific, and I whistle a tiny tune. A killer's work is never done, but even a killer deserves some rest. I hear they make good moonshine around here.

#

You ever coppice a tree, Jack? You ever cut a bedraggled willow to watch twice as many stalks come back, straighter and stronger than before? You ever see a cathedral of wood growing in some abandoned glade, with moss and sunlight all around, centered on a lonely stump? What you cut grows back tenfold.

We see you, Jack the Giant Killer, as we surround you. What you don't know about redwoods, will fill the ocean.

GHOST FOREST
Mark Wheaton

Vati turns off the car engine and we roll to a stop alongside the wheat field. The headlights have been off since we exited the highway, and Bernard and I are in the backseat, praying we aren't being followed. It's the last new moon of summer, and the faint starlight casts the field in a dark blue that only turns black when it reaches the forest beyond.

Those woods, the *Gespensterwald* (Ghost Forest), are notoriously immune to light. This is due to the thick canopy overhead created by the tens of thousands of white-trunked beech trees that give the forest its name. The dense thicket looms in the distance like a great wall of black, dividing earth and sky.

We wait. No one passes on the old dirt road. No lights come on in the distant farmhouses. After five minutes pass, Vati opens the passenger side door—the one door on the ancient Trabant that doesn't creak—and steps into the warm night, the heat of the late summer day lingering well past midnight. It wouldn't be so uncomfortable if we weren't padded within three layers of clothing.

"You'll be happy for the layers when we reach the sea," Vati says, as if reading my mind.

Satisfied no one's around, he waves for us to follow, and Bernard and I crawl into the front seat, then out of the car. The air smells of burning hay.

"What is that?" Bernard asks, wrinkling his nose.

"Cooking fire," Vati says. "Probably campers closer to Rostock."

A lie. Vati picked this spot to enter the Ghost Forest because the farmer—rather than give up his 200 acres to the East German government to be divided into several smaller, cooperative farms—

slaughtered his family, burned his fields, and then killed himself. He is not the first to do so.

What it means for us is this: no one is here to work the harvest on neighboring farms. No one is here to see us abandon our car and disappear into the woods.

"We go straight north through the woods," Vati says, checking his compass against a faded pre-war map in the dim light. "The boat is buried within the tree line on the other side. Then it's down to the beach and into the sea. Dawn is six hours away. We should be on the water in two."

He makes it sound like child's play.

"Then row to Denmark?" Bernard asks.

"Not all the way, as it would take days," Vati says, plucking a signal flare from his knapsack. "That's what this is for. We just have to reach the sea lanes and signal one of the morning ferries between Travemünde and Malmö. They'll take us the rest of the way."

Though Travemünde is in West Germany and Malmö in Sweden, Vati plans for us to seek asylum in Denmark, having heard they give the most government assistance to refugees. He has also long admired their railroads. As a railroad inspector himself, he hopes to find a job with the Danish State Railway.

For me, I don't care where we go, as long as it's nowhere people live in a constant state of unease. Nowhere young people are forced to accept uniformity designed to tamp down what makes them individuals, instead of dressing and acting as they do in the western magazines Vati sometimes finds on trains. Nowhere in which life's opportunities are decided by the state. Nowhere a person is conditioned to suspect their own verbal missteps or unpatriotic thoughts and question those of others.

I want a life without fear, or no life at all.

Vati shoulders the knapsack and takes Bernard's hand. I wish he'd take mine, too, but I'm the older sister. I have to be brave for my brother.

As we step through the scorched field, my gaze fixes on the impenetrable woods ahead. The trunks of the beeches, barely a meter or two apart, rise from the ground like the marble columns of an ancient temple. Or better yet, the fossilized ribcage of a great, prehistoric serpent. They have no branches until the very top, giving them a denuded, skeletal appearance. Then, at their peak, they open like an umbrella, sending thick, leafy branches in all directions, creating an interwoven ceiling of limbs and leaves with their neighbors.

They use this to hoard rainwater and block out the sun. Nothing grows in the Ghost Forest except the beech trees. No shrubs, no flowers, no vines, nor grass. The ground is covered with stones, moss, and a few mushrooms.

A dog barks in the distance. Vati hurls us to the ground and throws his body over ours. We are as still as the stars. There is no second bark. No shout from a border guard patrol. No rifle shot.

"Do you think Mrs. Schraeder called the police?" Bernard whispers.

Mrs. Schraeder, who lives down the hall from us in our apartment on Steepenweg, is one of our building's most notorious busybodies. Her floors creak and peephole darkens when anyone passes. Not that she singles us out. Spying on one's neighbor in the GDR is practically the national pastime.

"No, no," Vati says. "We left early, remember? Carrying a picnic basket? She would have no reason to suspect us."

There's another reason no one would think our midweek outing out of the ordinary. It's the one-year anniversary of the death of my mother. One year since the state's finest doctors failed her during what was meant to be a routine operation. One year since my father brought us home from the hospital and began bitterly plotting our escape to the West.

I glance back to our abandoned car. Vati isn't sentimental about it, but it makes me recall trips my mother took us on while he was away at work. Driving us along the Tollensesee or to the spruce forests at Hainich, singing along to Strauss operas on the car's barely functional radio as she battled the car's gearshift. One more piece of her we were leaving behind.

"Incredible," Vati says when we reach the towering beeches.

Dark, I think, staring beyond them into the unlit interior.

Vati removes a ball of twine from the knapsack, passes it through his belt loops, then hands it to me. I do the same, then pass it to Bernard. He has a little trouble, so I kneel in front of him, knotting it to his belt. When finished, we look like a trio of mountaineers.

Vati then hands us each a flashlight, black crepe banded around the lenses to dim their glow. When he'd slipped out here alone to bury the boat at the last new moon, passing not through the forest but slipping away from a railway depot near Nienhagen, he'd come across plenty of patrols on the cliffs overlooking the sea, including a guard tower overlooking the beach. But as far as he could tell, these patrols never ventured into the Ghost Forest.

"I painted the trees closest to where the boat is buried with phosphorescent paint," he reminds us. "It'll be invisible until hit with the flashlight beams. Don't remove the crepe until we're through the woods. Now, are we ready?"

I nod. Bernard hesitates.

"The sooner we start, the sooner we'll be done," Vati says. "And our first stop? Tivoli Gardens."

Bernard's eyes light up. He'd been terrified about living in the West up until the moment Vati found an old guidebook to Copenhagen's world-famous amusement park, Tivoli Gardens. The handful of faded photographs of the rides and attractions had captured Bernard's imagination.

"Okay," Bernard says. "Let's go."

The woods are unnerving from the first step. The trunks that glowed pale white moments before now vanish before us, swallowed up by darkness a few meters from the forest's edge. Our muted flashlight beams barely illuminate our feet. It becomes so pitch dark in every direction that it no longer feels like we're in a forest—it's as if we've descended into a salt mine or are trapped in the hull of some enormous ship.

It is as terrifying as it is disorienting. The sound of my father's footsteps marching resolutely ahead alone gives me comfort.

People mostly attempt to escape the GDR via three routes. There is the frontier between East and West Germany, but it is heavily patrolled and brimming with landmines. There is the Berlin Wall, but it is guarded by snipers. A few months ago, yet another young man trying to escape was shot and left to bleed to death under the barbed wire. Vati tried to keep this news from us, but I heard about it at school. His name was Peter. He was only three years older than me.

The third route is across the Baltic Sea. Some try to swim, hoping to avoid the patrols and make it to West German beaches. Most drown. Some try to escape by boat, but there are patrol ships and very few unguarded coastal spots to launch even a kayak. This is why my father chose to travel through the Ghost Forest; it is one of the few places almost no one attempts to breech.

As famous as it is for its white beech trees, it's also known as a labyrinth capable of confusing and trapping all who enter. Hikers don't emerge for weeks, getting turned around by the sameness of everything. Some don't emerge at all. During the war, two Red Army companies penetrated the woods to hunt for game. They were never heard from again.

Getting through the woods was only half the challenge. The other half is the boat itself.

Rather than raise suspicion by purchasing one, Vati hunted down the blueprints for a late nineteenth century collapsible lifeboat, the kind used by freighters and passenger liners. It took several months. He milled the wood himself, hand-tooled the ribs, struts, keel, and cut the canvas. It has survived test runs in placid lakes and rough rivers.

Now, it must survive a single voyage on the sea.

The twine between myself and Vati goes slack.

"What's wr—" I begin to say.

His hand flies to my lips. "Shh," he whispers.

Bernard bumps into me. I reach back and keep him from falling.

"Flashlights off," Vati whispers.

We obey. The darkness is made complete. The trees, so close seconds before, could be either near enough to touch or a kilometer in the distance.

Something moves in the forest. It is large and lumbering, its footfalls heavy against the stony ground. Its breath escapes in snorts. A bear, I think. It's impossible to pinpoint where the sounds come from. It could be anywhere around us.

"Don't move," Vati whispers.

As if I could move.

I try to remember what I learned in Young Pioneers. If a bear is near a house, you make a lot of noise to scare it away. It knows it doesn't belong there and will run. If you're in its territory, you acknowledge its presence and cautiously move on. You don't try to intimidate it or flee. Of course, these rules change if there are cubs.

There's no telling if this bear is a sow or boar.

It brushes against me. I almost fall down. It feels huge—the size of a car. I reach back for Bernard but cannot find his hand.

"*Gnh*," Vati groans.

Something hits the ground. Something *heavy*.

"Vati!" I cry, squatting low.

"Stay still," he says, as if from under the earth. "Stay. Still."

Cloth rips. Vati groans in pain. Somewhere behind me, Bernard shrieks.

"Vati!" Bernard shouts.

A new scent reaches my nose. It's...

Strawberries?

Cake?

Our food. The bear hasn't torn into my father, but our knapsack.

"Stay quiet," Vati says, voice trembling.

Time slows as the animal methodically tears through wax paper wrappings and devours the meal we were to eat at sea. Sweat pours down my face and arms. My muscles soon ache. I count the seconds, staving off the need to sit or even shift my weight.

"Käthe," Vati finally says. "It's gone."

Father turns on his flashlight, removes the crape, and arcs the beam over the ground. The knapsack's outer pocket is shredded. The rest is intact. What looks like strawberry jam stains the straps. Upon closer inspection, I see it's blood.

"You're hurt," I say.

"It's nothing."

I snatch away the flashlight and aim it at the wound. The bear's claws dug through his flesh, all the way to the bone. "We have to get you to a hospital."

"We have a first aid kit. You can stitch me up once we're in the boat. Where's Bernard?"

I aim the flashlight behind me. "Bernard?"

No answer.

"It's okay now, Bernard!" Vati calls out. "The bear is gone!"

I pull in the twine. It's snapped, and the end is frayed. I didn't feel it when it happened.

"Bernard!" I cry, louder now, my voice echoing through the trees. "Bernard!"

I spy a fast-moving silhouette in the woods. It's not Bernard, but the bear again. It charges straight for us. I barely have time to react when Vati lunges for me. I think he meant to push me aside, except it's too late. The beast slams into us at full speed. I go flying.

When I hit the ground, I pause to collect myself, figuring the worst is over. I rise to my feet to see a scene straight out of a nightmare.

The bear is cornered amongst three beech trees. It rears onto its back legs, pawing at the air in anger. The jagged shadows thrown up behind it make it look even bigger than it is. Embedded in its belly are two thin lances made from beechwood. Hemp ropes trail away from them, back to the largest stag I've ever seen, like something depicted on a medieval tapestry.

On its back rides an elderly woman, naked, except for a large bear skin. Over her eyes, she wears World War II-era night goggles like some kind of mad tank driver.

"*Schnell!*" she yells. "*Töte sie!*"

Four men emerge from behind the stag carrying lances. Their skin is pale and bruised, cut in places, rotten in others. Their eyes are gray and unseeing. The old woman directs them with taps from the end of a long reed she uses like a riding crop.

"My God," Vati says as the men surge toward the bear. "*Nachzehrer.*"

I stiffen. Nachzehrer are creatures akin to ghouls or vampires. They rise from the grave after death. Unlike vampires, they don't drink blood to stay alive. They eat corpses.

Also, they're not real. They're fairy tales.

The men wear tattered clothes over their rotting bodies and are practically naked save for strips of cloth around their wrists, necks, and ankles. One appears to be clothed in the remains of a military uniform that looks over a century old. Like a costume in a play.

They press in close to the weakening bear. Blood sluices through its lower jaw onto its chin, likely the result of a punctured lung. It swipes wearily at them. When one of the undead gets too close, however, the bear seizes the opportunity and sinks its teeth into the hunter's throat. The stricken victim does not cry out. It barely fights back even as the bear tears his head from his body.

Two others grab the bear's forearms and yank them backward, knocking the animal off-balance. It stabs its claws into the chest of the one nearest as the last of the group drives a lance directly into its midsection. Once deep inside its belly, the hunter jerks the sharpened branch downward until the bear's intestines spit out of its body and splash onto the ground. The fight goes out of the great beast. It sinks to its knees. The old woman on the stag barks out another order, and her accomplices drag the dying bear onto a travois behind her mount. The decapitated man and its head are added to the pile.

To my horror, the head stares back at me even as the bear's blood washes down its face in sheets. The ghoul's mouth opens and closes methodically, revealing blackened teeth and a desiccated tongue. It tries to speak, but it can't vocalize any words, having lost the use of its lungs.

The old woman follows its gaze, lowering the night vision goggles to stare at me and my father. Her lips curl up into a snarl and she points. "Grab them!"

"Run!" Vati yells.

I dash away. Despite the flashlight in my hand, I can barely see ahead of me. I slam into a beech trunk, spin away, then hit a second one. I fear the light will attract the... what? The nachzehrer? The witch who is their master? Am I ready to call them that?

So, I switch the light off, and I swim deeper into the oily blackness, feeling as if I'm sinking farther down into the ocean than light could ever travel. Though I'm running, I get the feeling of being aloft. Of falling. Of flying. I can't tell earth from sky. The silence is as isolating as the darkness. The only noise is what I make myself, right now... my erratic footsteps and the thunder of my galloping heartbeat.

I picture my father a few steps behind me, though I cannot hear him, and I fear he's not there. I imagine my mother there instead, alive and healthy, holding my brother's hand. Her voice whispers that this is a dream. That it's almost over. That I will soon be free.

Then I hear my name for real.

"Käthe...? Käthe...?"

I wonder if I've gone mad. Is the voice in my mind? Or is it from the night?

"Vati...?" the darkness asks again.

It's Bernard. He's scared. Mournful. I'm about to call out when I spy a dull, flickering light in the forest. I flatten myself against the ground and peer up at it. It's about fifty meters away, winding in and around the tree trunks.

As it draws closer, the light is revealed as not a single candle but four lanterns held aloft by these mysterious nachzehrer as they move through the forest. Amidst their undead horde strides another giant stag, as large as the Trojan Horse. Swinging between its thick antlers is a wicker cage.

Inside is Bernard.

"Käthe...?" he calls, hands gripping the wicker bars. "Vati...?"

His voice is airy, as if he doesn't really want us to hear. He fears for our lives as much as his own. So I shadow the procession. I don't know how, but I must help him escape.

Something flutters in the trees overhead. A bat? A bird? It comes to rest directly above me, barely visible in the dim light of the nachzehrer's lanterns. It's a nightingale. It cocks its head and flits its wings.

Then speaks.

"There you are," it says as if spoken from inside a great cavern.

Half a dozen of the nachzehrer emerge from the woods around me carrying ropes and lances. Their bodies are so pale they blend right in with the beech trees.

The nightingale grows larger and loses its feathers, transforming into the old woman. She climbs down the tree trunk face-first, drawing her tongue across her lips like a toad.

"You have nothing to fear, *tochter*," she says, touching my cheek with a bony hand. "Nothing to fear from Frau Holle."

Before I can demand that she never call me *daughter* in German again, the nachzehrer shove a cloth in my mouth and bind my wrists and ankles.

#

"Käthe?"

I open my eyes. Had I been unconscious? It is lighter here, though not from the coming of day. I'm in a clearing, the Ghost Forest's canopy parting to allow in starlight. Rather than a field, however, the break in the trees hosts an undulating, sulfurous bog. Several trees seem to have sunk into it over time, their decaying upper branches still jutting up through the bog's surface, suggesting a depth of several meters.

Bernard is still caged above the stag's antlers, like an insect caught in a spider's web. Around him in the woods are dozens—if not hundreds—of the undead nachzehrer, their pale bodies blending in next to the beech trees. More stags stand alongside them.

My gag has been removed and my bindings cut, yet I am surrounded. There is nowhere for me to go.

"Are you hurt, Bernard?" I ask.

"No. But... who are these people?"

"Kidnappers. Criminals."

"Do not lie to him, *tochter*," a voice oozes from somewhere in the dark. "You trespass in my woods, and now you slander me? How impolite."

"We are not trespassing," I say, searching the darkness for the witch. "We are simply trying to get to the sea. To escape this place."

"My dear, no one escapes this place."

A nightingale flutters over to land on one of the exposed branches rising from the bog. It transforms into the old woman. She looks from me to Bernard.

"You have a choice to make, *kinder*," she says. "I offer it to all who come to my woods. Enter the bog and join me here in eternal life, or leave this world now, gifting your flesh to my cohort."

The nachzehrer smack their lips hungrily at this suggestion. I can't imagine a worse choice—become an undead monster, or be devoured by one.

I scan the woods, feeling in my bones that my father is within the trees, plotting our escape. I can feel his presence. I can—

His knapsack. It leans against a tree close to Bernard's stag, as if left behind to collect later. Is he already here? Already making his move?

"Ach, *ja*," Frau Holle says, following my gaze. "*Dein Vater.* You await his guidance, yet he has already made his choice. He begged for us to accept him in exchange for safe passage for you. But that... that is not how it works."

I go rigid. "What're you saying?"

She raises a bony finger. Two nachzehrer emerge from the woods and walk directly into the bog. They are up to their waists in the muck after four steps, disappearing completely after six more. Can they possibly breathe under there? Or did Frau Holle so easily send her minions to a permanent grave?

My questions are answered a second later when the ghouls surface, their heads dripping with mud and moss. They lead a third figure between them.

I scream.

It is the loudest sound I have ever made. It barely articulates my anguish.

The figure is my father.

He is covered in peat moss and mud. It drips from his hair and clothing and even from his mouth. Thin lines of mud pour down his nose like tears. His eyelids droop open to reveal a pair of unseeing eyes.

"Vati!" Bernard yells. "Vati!"

If my father hears him, he makes no indication.

"What have you done to him?" I shout at Frau Holle.

"What have *I* done? This was his choosing."

"You're a monster!"

"I am merely the last of my kindred. All the others, every last one, dead at the hands of intruders to our woods."

"We meant you no harm! We didn't even know you were here!"

"Your ignorance is meant to move me?"

My father steps from the bog onto dry land. He is not pale yet like the other nachzehrer. His clothes are intact, as is his flesh. If I hadn't witnessed him emerge from under the peat, I might think him as being alive. Maybe having fallen in the water by accident.

But I know what a corpse looks like. How the light is gone from the eyes. How immediately shrunken the body is absent an animating soul. Whatever stands in my father's clothes is separate and apart from the man I once knew. He is simply gone.

"Vati...?" Bernard asks. "Why don't you speak?"

"He has joined my nachzehrer," Frau Holle says. "You are welcome to do the same."

Bernard's eyes widen.

"Don't you want to be with your father again?" she asks. "You will never be far from his side. You will never fear nor ever worry again. I will protect you, always. I will be your new mother."

For a second, I fear Bernard will agree. Then he shakes his head violently and pounds on the bars of his cage. "No, I won't join you! Never, ever! Let me go!"

Frau Holle angers. "He has made his choice. He is yours to devour!'

The stag lowers its antlers, bringing Bernard down to the nachzehrer. They fly at his cage, tearing it open as his terrified squeals echo through the forest.

"Stop!" I yell. "Stop right now!"

Frau Holle raises a finger. The nachzehrer freeze. Bernard sinks into the back of the cage, body heaving with sobs.

"We will join you, Frau Holle," I whisper. "Together. Let me go to him."

"If you mean trickery—"

"We have lost our mother and now our father. There is no life for us anymore."

She stares at me for a long moment, then assents. The nachzehrer move aside, allowing me to walk to my brother's cage.

"I don't want to go into the bog," Bernard says. "I want to go home. I want to go to school in the morning. I don't want to be like them."

"It's okay, Bernard," I say, taking his hand to guide him out of the cage and to the bog. "Frau Holle will protect us. You heard her."

He tentatively steps out, staring into the peat. Frau Holle transforms back into a nightingale and flutters over to sit atop his cage.

"Go on," she says. "All the way in."

"Will it hurt?" Bernard asks.

"You won't feel a thing," Frau Holle insists.

"Neither will you," I say.

"What's that?" Frau Holle asks.

It's too late. I've looped Vati's knapsack strap around my foot. I drop to one knee, yank the knapsack over, and grab the signal flare from inside. The nachzehrer lunge forward as I aim it at the tiny nightingale.

"You think you can harm me with that?" the nightingale chirps. "In my own forest?"

"I don't think that at all."

I trigger the flare. It ignites and blasts directly past the nightingale. The flare flies into the sky, leaving a trail of sparks in its wake. When it's higher than the trees, it explodes, lighting up the night with the brightness of a thousand stars.

Just as I anticipated, the stags panic, stomping their massive hooves and swinging their heads. The nachzehrer grab at their reins, but the great beasts buck and slam their antlers into the nearest beech trunks. Trees and ghouls alike are flung into the bog.

"Let's go!" I say, grabbing Vati's knapsack.

Bernard doesn't move. He stares at our father standing motionless at the bog's edge.

"Vati?" Bernard says. "Can you hear me? Are you in there?"

He turns to us, staring back with his unseeing eyes.

"Bernard, he's gone..."

"No, he recognizes me," Bernard says. "Can't you see?"

He offers his hand.

"Come with us, Vati," Bernard says. "Come with us to the sea."

Vati slowly lifts his hand as well. Mud and peat ooze off of it, dripping on the ground as he reaches out to Bernard.

Before I can shout a warning, Vati lunges for Bernard's outstretched hand. But he misses and stumbles to the ground in a heap. It's possible he tried to miss on purpose, as one last act of defiance against Frau Holle. Or maybe he was getting used to his new body after being drowned and resurrected in the bog. I can't really say for certain.

A new sound echoes through the trees; it comes from above and sounds like the flapping wings of some great dragon. A searchlight's beam cuts through the canopy. A military helicopter. It hovers over the clearing, its lights scattering the nachzehrer in all directions.

"Come on," I say, tugging at Bernard's arm. "He's gone!"

We return to the darkness.

#

Once we've gone several meters, I take out Vati's flashlight and compass. I have no idea how far we have veered off course, or how soon it is until dawn.

"This way," I say, pointing through the gloom.

We slog ahead past seemingly endless trees. Despite the compass assuring me we are on the right track, it feels like a trick. Like we're walking in circles. How would we even know?

My body, overwhelmed with fatigue, wants to collapse. My mind, to scream. If I think about what happened to Vati, I won't be able to take another step. I try to envision our lives in Denmark. It's impossible without our father.

"What's that, Käthe?" Bernard asks, clutching my hand tighter.

Up ahead, something glows. I fear it's one of the nachzehrer's lanterns, yet it doesn't flicker. I turn off the flashlight, and it vanishes. After a couple of cautious steps, I turn the light back on. Tiny, dull green splotches of phosphorescent paint on four different tree trunks glow to life.

Vati's handiwork. The boat must be close.

I move the flashlight's beam from tree to tree, and a path forms through the forest. The paint splotches are initially on a number of trees. The trail narrows the further north we walk until there is paint on only one tree. It's in the shape of an arrow pointing down.

"It's here," I whisper to Bernard.

We drop to our knees and find several rocks piled in front of the trunk with recently turned earth underneath. I scoop the soil away in great handfuls, digging deeper and deeper until my fingers touch the canvas shroud protecting the boat. I carefully dig out the rest of the dirt, not wanting to damage the boat when I pull it from the ground.

It's so heavy I can barely lift it. Once it's out from its temporary grave, I look inside to make sure it's in one piece. It looks as it did the moment Vati finished it in his workshop. Our homemade method of escape.

"Now, it's past the guards, down to the beach, then the sea and freedom," I say to Bernard. "As Vati wanted."

He nods and picks up the back of the boat. I turn off the flashlight. The darkness recedes. The beech trunks in front of us are silhouetted against a backdrop of stars.

We half-carry, half-drag the boat to the tree line and find ourselves staring out over the sea. The stars are reflected on the dark surface of the water, making it look as if we've reached not merely the edge of the woods, but the edge of the world.

A new, much brighter light swings past. The searchlight from the guard tower. We duck low as it passes. It illuminates the narrow trail that runs along the cliff between the forest and the cliff face, as well as the stairs leading to the beach below.

They are maybe three dozen meters away.

"Remember, we wait for a guard patrol to pass, count off three minutes, then go to the stairs," I say, repeating instructions Vati drilled into us. "The hard part will be paddling past the breakers. Once we've done that, we're safe and on our way."

Bernard looks down.

"What is it?" I ask.

"He's all alone."

I take Bernard's hands in mine. "Berni, he's gone. He's gone to be with Mutter."

"He's not dead. Not really. He's trapped here. So, he can't be with her."

As soon as he says it, I know I will never have a satisfactory answer for this.

"It will be okay," I say.

He's about to protest further when we hear voices. Two border guards, machine guns slung over their shoulders, and a German shepherd out ahead of them on a leash. They speak in hushed tones. It's the dog I fear. I wait for it to raise its snout, to isolate our scent from all others in the forest. To turn its head and bark.

Instead of any of those things, it simply passes us by.

I silently count off 180 seconds as the guards disappear, and then I lift my end of the boat. Bernard follows me out of the woods, allowing his end of the boat to drag. We let the guard tower's searchlight pass and then hurry toward the stairs. They look steep and treacherous from this height. If we slip carrying the bulky boat, we could break our necks. But a cooling breeze blows up to us from the Baltic, bringing with it the tang of salt and the promise of freedom on the other side. The beach looks empty and the sea gentle. It's low tide. We are so close now.

"*Halt! Hände hoch!*"

Bright lantern light blinks over us. A second patrol has slipped behind us, their guard dog straining at the leash. Bernard drops his end of the boat and raises his hands. I refuse to let go.

"Put it on the ground or we'll shoot," one guard says while his partner speaks into a radio.

I still won't let go. We've come too far and lost too much.

And then—movement from the tree line.

"Pick up the boat," I whisper to Bernard.

"What?"

"Quiet!" the guard yells. His dog's attention turns from us to the woods. It yips and barks, but the guards ignore it.

"Get ready," I whisper.

This time, Bernard picks up the boat. The guard, furious, fires three shots into the air. It draws the attention of the nachzehrer, and they pour from the woods as one, teeth bared and lances at the ready. The guards react almost instantly, firing their weapons point blank. The combined muzzle flash lights up the woods, revealing hundreds of ghouls surging forward as one.

The bullets shred flesh and tear away limbs, but the nachzehrer keep coming.

"Let's go!" I yell to Bernard over the cacophony.

We drag the boat to the stairs as fast as we can manage. The old boards creak under our weight, and the boat threatens to slide away from us, but adrenaline makes us surefooted. Thundering rifle shots join the machine gun fire. Snipers in the tower.

I wonder if our father is among the nachzehrer. More than that, I wonder if any part of him knows that he saved our lives.

We finally reach the sand and drag the boat as close to the water as possible. I strip off the shroud and open up the boat like a folding fan. Once the hull is fully expanded, the canvas between its hinged ribs taut, I bang the struts into place to keep it unfurled. Last are the three flat wooden pieces that double as braces and seats. We bang them into the slots my father skillfully cut in the matching struts. Then we stand back and admire our hard work.

Every smooth edge, every oiled and working hinge, is the doing of our father. I wish he were here to see his handiwork in action.

"There!" Bernard shouts.

I squint up at the clifftop battle.

Vati and several other ghouls wrestle a weapon away from one of the guards. They toss it and its screaming owner over the side to the beach below.

I turn away. "Let's get this in the water and get out of here."

"We can't leave him!"

"You want his sacrifice to mean nothing?"

He shakes his head. And together, we shove the boat into the water, climb in, and grab the oars from below the seats. We paddle straight into the oncoming waves, but get pushed back each time, water coursing over us. It's when I remember to turn the boat slightly and approach the waves at an angle that we crest the first one.

"Come on, Bernard! A few more like that. Push hard!"

"I am, I am!"

One final swell rolls toward us before the sea grows calmer on the other side. It moves fast and rises high, as if determined to smash our tiny boat to splinters.

"Row as hard as you can!" I order.

Bernard does and we speed toward the wave. As the bow rises, I switch sides with my oar and angle us along the crest. We shudder. We're lifted. And then we slide into relatively more tranquil water.

"We did it, Bernard!" I yell. "We did it!"

I expect a cheer. But I receive only silence.

I turn to find Bernard slumped over his oar, a dark stain spreading across the back of his shirt.

"Bernard!" I cry, grabbing his arm to lift him up.

It's a bullet wound. The guard tower sniper.

"Hang on, Berni," I say, grabbing the first aid kit from Vati's knapsack. Except there's too much bleeding to be staunched. He is fading, fast.

I tilt my head back and wail in anguish. I throw my arms around my brother, the tremendous weight of the tragedy enveloping my heart. I can barely breathe. I look back to the guard tower and wave my arms.

"I'm right here! Take me next!"

Something moves through the air. I pray for a bullet. But it is the nightingale. It lands behind Bernard, stares at me for a moment, then transforms into Frau Holle.

"It's not too late," she says, touching Bernard's forehead. "He can still join his father in the woods. You're welcome, too. But only if you choose to turn back."

I stare at her in horror and then look back toward the Ghost Forest. The fighting has ended. The nachzehrer now stare out over the sea in silence. Waiting.

I touch Bernard's hand, and I see all the blood. So much blood. His eyes are glazing over, his life almost gone. But he nods to me.

He makes his choice. And I make mine.

I carefully lift Bernard out of the boat and place him in the water. I kiss him lovingly on the forehead, something I often did when he was an infant. Then I watch as the tide slowly carries him back to shore, where Frau Holle now waits for him alongside several of the nachzehrer. They lift him from the water, carry him up the stairs, and disappear into the woods.

Once they are gone, I paddle out to sea until my arms ache and my hands are torn and bloody. I have no tears left. I have no food or water. I think of my mother and father, and I think of poor Bernard. I cannot fathom a life without them, though I will have to.

I paddle on, knowing I must try.

ONE RED SHOE
Scott Paul Hallam

A **hundred** pale shades of Davie lay on our glass coffee table. One year ago today, we lost him right outside our home, nestled in the crook of the Allegheny National Forest. I poured over these photographs while my husband Leonard sat on the couch opposite me, not looking up from his work laptop, scotch on the rocks in hand.

Our living room was an amalgam of chrome and glass. No socks on the floor. No rings of water on the table. The smell of artificial lemon diffused in the air. A pristine facade juxtaposed the war-torn streets crumbling inside of me.

On the table, faded images of me in a hospital gown, a swaddled newborn in my arms. A little boy with an untucked shirt in front of a school, his hair mussed by the wind. A blurry image of Davie kicking a soccer ball.

I turned to Leonard. His eyes never raised past his screen.

A warmth swam over my body; sparks of color danced at the edges of my vision. I needed to get out of this room, away from this self-inflicted torture.

I pulled open the sliding glass door that led into our backyard. Our own little *Walden*. Memories floated back to the autumn day when the realtor brought us to see the place, a large pond in the middle of the woods, rows of maple and pine—an oasis away from the city life that had suffocated us.

Memories now tainted, remembrances of boots, dozens of them, trampling every inch of ground, hoping to find a hat, a toy, a muddy sweatshirt. But I never joined the search. Sure, I had lunch and dinner and hot coffee ready for the volunteers and police officers, but I couldn't bring myself to enter the forest where there was even a chance that I'd find his body, cold and blue under a pile of rotting leaves. I hadn't entered the woods since.

We had heard the stories. Urban legends about spirits that supposedly haunted the nearby forest. We listened to the news reports of two teenage boys found frozen to death underneath a cluster of pines after a night of underage drinking. But we dismissed the stories as either exaggerations or happenstance. We loved the clean air in our lungs and the spacious yard where we built a swing set for Davie. And dismissive we remained, until tragedy struck home.

The night was now pregnant with stars, with a waning crescent that sliced the sky open, pouring moonlight onto the snow-covered ground. The snow fell in white clumps.

I looked out into the blackness and heard something, a high-pitched whisper, something recognizable but muted on the wind that whipped through the trees.

I pulled my cell phone from my jeans pocket and flicked on the flashlight app, scanning our yard for a raccoon or coyote or some other animal invading our homestead. The swath of yellow light swept across our property, highlighting the skeletal remains of trees iced with snow. The light didn't reflect off of the eyes of a stray cat or dog, but glinted off something else, a dark object in a sea of white.

I moved toward the thing in the snow, shining the light directly on it. My heart fluttered, and I couldn't catch my breath. Lying in the yard was a tennis shoe made of red canvas. A left foot shoe. It was Davie's.

I shouted for Leonard, and he came running out, leather jacket in hand. I still couldn't form words, just continued to train the light on the shoe. He approached and slowed his pace. When he looked down, I could tell from his face that he knew exactly what it meant.

On day three of the search last year, in a patch of snow-covered plants, a volunteer had found a red tennis shoe. Davie's. But the right one. No other evidence. No blood, no DNA, not even a stray hair. Just a shoe.

Not a body in the lake, or a corpse mutilated by a bear or cougar. No evidence of an abduction, either, although that's what I believe happened.

Just a little boy who had vanished.

I shifted my cell phone's light toward the mouth of the woods, the red tennis shoe in my left hand, and we inched forward, Leonard so close to me I could smell the scotch on his breath. I didn't want to enter those dark woods. Ghost-like memories resided there.

As I paused, a murmur seemed to carry itself on the frigid winds that blew across our property. Not an animal cry, but a voice, unintelligible, but also unmistakable.

"Davie?" I asked, fragile at first, then louder. "Davie, is that you?"

"It's not him Susan," Leonard said. "The shoe, these sounds... on tonight of all nights? Someone is trying to fuck with us. Call the cops."

Leonard, his voice hoarse, boomed but also wavered. He heard it too; I know he did. The same timbre, the same way Davie used to elongate his S's. A mother doesn't forget, not entirely. Neither does a father. And if Leonard and I were going insane, we were going insane together.

"No, Leonard. I don't know what's going on, but that's Davie's voice. I'm going in to find out."

He tried to grab my arm, but I twisted away, noticing his face shadowed by darkness, the cell phone light splashing against his body. He didn't speak, but he pulled his hand away from me.

Inside my mind, rage warred with hope. But as I looked at Leonard, the man I loved, or had once loved, my spirit melted a bit. I thought back to when he used to wrap his arms around me after a long day at work. For a moment, rage lost the battle.

In some ways, I pitied him. One year ago, he was the one watching Davie while I was on another business trip across the country. A game of hide and seek gone wrong. Laughter and smiles one second, then not even a body to bury the next.

When I looked at Leonard, his square jawline, his wind-blown brown hair, I saw Davie. My thoughts tumbled back to memories of last year, when our yard was coated in snow like tonight, and we built snowmen all over the backyard like Davie wanted. We built so many that we went through an entire bag of carrots that we used for their noses. I've tried to hang onto that fuzzy image of Davie smiling as we built snowman after snowman, tried to keep his voice cradled inside my head. Images and sounds that have kept me alive these past twelve months.

Leonard and I entered the woods through an opening partially obscured by branches that hung low, as if wanting to hold in all of the forest's secrets. We wound our way through the narrow trail that was once so familiar, so well traveled. We stepped over rotted logs in our path, the branches closer than ever before, the wind roaring in our ears as snow assaulted our cheeks and eyes. A shiver ran through me; I had forgotten my coat, while Leonard had his jacket on, zipped up tight.

We turned a corner at a large rock formation and almost collided with a fawn. I yelped and jumped back, locking eyes with it, my cell phone's light pointing in its direction. Even though dense snowflakes plummeted to the ground, I could still see the fawn's faint white spots. The mother couldn't be far.

For a few moments, no one moved. Not me, not Leonard, and not the fawn. I had a crazy, fleeting thought to ask if it had seen my son. Then it bolted in the opposite direction, off the trail and down the hill.

By instinct, I took off after it, feeling that our meeting wasn't accidental, that Davie was somewhere in these woods and somehow trying to communicate with us. The branches clawed at my face, drawing blood, ripping at my cashmere sweater. Leonard was right beside me, beating his arms against the branches that seemed to grasp at our skin.

We staggered down the hill to a small clearing. The fawn was there, nibbling at something in the snow. As it raised its head again, it wasn't the face of a newly born deer, but Davie's face: his blue eyes, his wavy brown hair, his freckled cheeks.

I screamed and dropped my phone. The woods turned dark, and I scrambled for the light, lifting the phone once more to the fawn still staring at us with Davie's face.

I thought my eyes were liars, and I didn't know what was happening. I approached the fawn slowly, not wanting to scare it off. Davie's eyes—the fawn's eyes—burned with electricity, and I was only ten feet away when another shape leaped out of the darkness.

A bobcat pounced on the fawn, tearing at its flesh.

The fawn fell, its pelt stained red with blood. Leonard lunged at the bobcat, which jumped out of the way and sprinted deeper into the woods.

My mind cracked in half. I didn't trust my own senses, and I didn't want to look, but I knew I had to. I trained the light of my phone on the torn and bloody flesh of the fawn, to its face.

But it wasn't Davie's face any longer. Just an animal's face, with lifeless black eyes.

Leonard and I turned toward one another. We didn't speak, we couldn't, but I think I caught tears welling up in his eyes. As the wind raged, we heard a voice again. Davie's voice, without a doubt. This time clear and bright.

"That wasn't me, Mommy—don't worry. I was just playing a prank. But I'm still mad at you. You were always away for work. And I'm still mad at you, Daddy. You were taking care of me, and you lost me. But don't stop now. Let's have more fun. You can't give up... you've got to find me!"

The voice ended as abruptly as it began. Leonard stumbled into a tree and grabbed the closest branch, ripping it free and hurling it down the trail. I couldn't hold back tears that streamed down my cheeks, warm on my skin. I'm not sure how, but Davie had to be alive. That voice. His and his alone.

My thoughts now raced, thinking back to when this hell began. Back then, I was the ambitious one. On the fast track in HR for a multinational engineering firm. I traveled. A lot. But I always called home, always heard Davie's voice before he went to bed.

After that night a year ago, all I wanted to do was find out what happened to him. I quit my job, worked with the police, even hired private investigators that did nothing more than deplete our savings. No leads. A cold case.

Leonard, on the other hand, immersed himself in work. He went back to work a week after Davie went missing. He worked late nights and traveled more than ever for his consulting firm, even earned a promotion three months ago.

I never stopped blaming myself for what happened that night. I should have been there. A mother should have been with her son.

We walked along in silence down the familiar trail that Leonard and I could have followed even without the light from the phone. The trail led to the large pond where we kept a small canoe moored to a makeshift dock.

"You know this makes no sense, Susan. I bet someone drugged us. We're tripping or something. It's not like it's a big secret that Davie went missing a year ago. Some fucking bastard is going to pay for this."

"We're seeing and hearing the same hallucinations, Leonard, so don't try to rationalize this like everything else. I know it doesn't make sense. But I know Davie's out here."

I brushed against Leonard's arm, and half of me wanted to grab on for dear life and not let go. The other half hated him for not even considering the possibility that Davie might still be alive in these woods, so close that we simply had to reach out and grab him.

Leonard stopped in the middle of the trail, crossing his arms, the snow falling on his shoulders.

"Call someone, Susan. The cops, your mom, anyone. Let's get some help out here."

"No. Go back if you want. If there is even a chance... I'm moving on."

I walked further down the path and looked up at the pinpricks in the sky. I could see the Big Dipper, the only asterism that Davie and I could point out. Leonard remained rooted to his spot, so I marched on.

As I walked down the trail, I heard the crackling of branches, the crunch of snow behind me. Leonard followed without speaking.

The trail widened and then spilled out into an opening. The pond stood right in front of us, moonlight shimmering off the water that resembled black glass. The smell of pine wafted from the trees that lined the pond.

The cell phone and the moon and stars were not the only illumination; a glowing figure, emitting blue light, stood at the far end of the pond, almost looking like it was hovering on the water. The figure looked like a child in a hoodie, a red hoodie, the one Leonard said Davie wore the night he disappeared.

Davie's voice boomed over the wind.

"You guys found me. But before you swim out to me, I think it's time Daddy tells you the truth, Mommy. The truth of what happened that night."

Davie's voice struck another invisible body blow to my chest, but the voice sounded rougher, angrier, sardonic even. I shook off the shock and shined the cell phone light—now at nine percent of power—right in Leonard's face. He backed away as if the light burned his skin, his mouth open, on the verge of saying something, but he didn't. It was Davie who spoke next.

"Come on Daddy, tell her. Tell her we weren't playing hide and seek at all. Tell her that."

"Tell me what, Leonard?" I said as I pushed him towards the lake with all of my might, still holding Davie's red shoe clutched in my hand. Acid crept up my throat. Even though I asked the question, I didn't want to hear the answer.

Leonard stumbled backwards and stuttered, mumbling his broken words, and at that moment, a stake was thrust into my heart again, because I knew Leonard's telltale signs; he was hiding something.

"Listen, Susan, I did nothing wrong, okay? I just, I..."

"Daddy, tell Mommy that you were too busy on your phone and drinking your beer that you didn't even notice I left the house. I asked you to play, and you said *no, not now, later*. You didn't even look up at me, Daddy, so I went outside. Tell Mommy you didn't even know I was gone for three whole hours."

I kept pushing Leonard as Davie's voice enveloped me, but I heard truth in the words, and I punched Leonard with both of my fists, knocking him back to the edge of the pond, the water now cascading over his leather boots.

"What the hell, Leonard! Is that true? Did you just ignore our son?"

He paused, eyes wide, pain etched into his every feature. He breathed deeply and then spoke.

"Yes, okay... it's true. But how the hell was I to know he'd drown or get taken or whatever the hell happened to him? This is sick.

Someone's trying to rip us apart, Susan. Someone wants money from us. That's all this is."

And in that moment, the last little part of my heart that still glowed soft and warm for Leonard, the part of me that loved the way he sang to me on our wedding day at the top of his lungs for all our guests to hear—that part of my heart callused over and darkened like the night sky.

I didn't know if I hated him for his neglect, for losing our little boy, or if I despised him more for denying that Davie was still alive.

"Screw you, Leonard, you asshole. Davie's out there. I can hear him, and I can see him on the other side of the pond. Let's go get our son."

I glanced back over the pond, and the glowing figure had disappeared. Davie was gone. The frigid wind bit into my cheeks. My cell phone battery held only a four percent charge, and I let the light fall on Leonard's face, a face scarred with guilt. And that's when I noticed the hands.

Hands rose out of the depths, grasping at Leonard's khakis, pulling him into the water. They clawed at his buttoned shirt and jacket—first a couple of hands, then three, then six—and Leonard tried to push them all away, but more rose from the black water, pulling him further into the pond until he went completely under. After a few seconds, he emerged from the icy darkness, gasping, thrashing about as the hands pulled him further into the depths of the pond.

I jumped into the water and started slapping them away, but more kept rising up. So many that I lost count.

At that moment, my phone died, and there was only darkness and the sound of Leonard struggling to stay afloat. He screamed my name, which echoed on the howling winds as the hands tore at my sweater and my flesh. I broke free, sprinting towards the hill that I knew emptied into the road that led out of the woods.

As I ran, Leonard's voice grew quieter, muffled, the splashing periodic. I made my way up the hill with the moon bathing me in pale light. My mind panicked, burning white hot; I tried not to think of what was happening to Leonard, just pure animal instinct pushing me to run, to survive.

I clambered up a steep incline, and instead of roots and plants to grasp onto, I grabbed objects that didn't feel right, that didn't belong in the middle of a forest. Rubber and canvas beneath my fingertips. The moon bathed the ground in wan light, confirming that a mound of Davie's red shoes—not one or two but hundreds, maybe thousands—covered the hill. Then I was sliding back down and falling into a morass of shoes.

I writhed and struggled to get my footing and finally found a way to climb higher. Laughter blasted my ears; a boy's giddy cackle.

As I ascended, I noticed a brighter light puncturing the darkness, making me tingle with anticipation. Maybe, just maybe, through all this madness, and through these horrible visions, I would finally get to see Davie in the flesh.

I scaled the mountain of tennis shoes, not knowing what was happening, not knowing Leonard's fate back in the pond, but I finally made my way to the crest of the hill that emptied into a road.

The light I saw as I climbed the hill emanated from a street lamp. I stood in the middle of the road, not sure where to go, waiting for Davie to say something, anything. Then I heard the roar of an engine.

I turned to see headlights barreling towards me, faster, getting closer, and I dove out of the way, falling back into the snow on the edge of the forest, and I heard screeching tires, the splash of slush, and as I looked up, I spied a white van that had stopped dead in front of me.

I rose to my feet, my shoulder aching where I had landed, and I didn't know what a van was doing out here at this time of night, in this neck of the woods, just parked there, but I recognized the van as the one I had seen in my nightmares.

In my reoccurring dreams this past year, dark arms reached out and stole Davie, throwing him into a white van, transporting him to God knows where. For countless hours, I lay awake at night thinking of nothing but this van and what some sick pervert did to my son in the back of it. The police couldn't confirm an abduction, but that seemed the only answer that ever made sense to me.

I cautiously approached the vehicle, which now shimmered in the light, coated with a thick layer of translucent ooze. As I stared at the van with dark-tinted windows, I heard a cacophony of engine noise, and I saw headlights flooding the road from both directions. I jumped to the side and hid behind a pine tree.

White vans barreled down the road, approaching from both the left and the right. Tires squealed from brakes being slammed down hard. Over a dozen vans now crammed the narrow country road.

A *thwack* sound echoed in the night as their sliding doors simultaneously slid open. I heard Davie's voice clear as a bell, saying that I had found him, that *everything will be okay Mommy, just please leave with me.* In the van closest to me, I could smell Davie—I never forgot his scent—and while I knew that this was insane, that nothing added up, I could still sense him around me as a hand emerged from the nearby van, reaching toward me. A boy's hand.

Davie's scent so intoxicated my mind that I barely noticed the roots growing from the tires and the undercarriage of the vehicles. The vines wrapped around the hood and side mirrors, transforming the vehicles into amorphous white pods that smelled of earth and decay.

But I ignored the images, because my son was waiting for me mere inches away. I reached out, grasping the tender flesh of his arm. And as I entered the gaping mouth of the van, it felt like a reuniting—a homecoming of sorts.

And then the van's shadow swallowed me whole, followed by the sound of a door sliding shut behind me.

#

From the moment Delores entered her daughter Susan's home, she felt the weight of ghosts crash in on her. Delores's husband Hank shuffled behind her in his gray sweatpants and Penn State T-shirt, ready to box up the lives that had all but vanished.

"I'll start upstairs and clear out the closets," her husband said. "You start in the kitchen." He growled each command, clutching unfolded cardboard boxes under each arm.

Delores still hadn't come to terms with her daughter's disappearance. That's why they had waited so long to clear out the house. She woke up every morning thinking today would be the day Susan and her family would waltz back into their home and reconvene their lives.

She was ever the optimist. Just like Susan.

Delores paced around the grey living room where a whiskey glass stood abandoned on the coffee table, untouched since the night Susan and Leonard disappeared. The police found no bodies, no articles of clothing, nothing except Susan's dead cell phone on the road behind the woods. No cars had been moved from the garage, no money taken from the house, and both passports were still inside their home safe. Just two people gone, like smoke dissipating into the night sky.

Delores didn't believe her family was dead. According to the police, they were still missing. There were no leads as of yet, but in her heart, she knew they were out there somewhere, maybe even locked in some sicko's basement. But they had to be alive, all three of them: Susan, Davie, and Leonard.

A warmth rose up from her stomach, and she gagged. Spots flashed across her eyes. She needed air. She opened up the door into the backyard now coated white with the first snow of the season. Heatless sunlight bathed the grounds, making the snow twinkle. A light breeze swayed the tall pines.

As Delores stared into the mouth of the forest, she heard a sound, low at first, then rising in pitch, coalescing into an audible form, clear and sharp.

"Mom, can you hear me? I found Davie. Leonard's here, too. But we're injured. Come help. Bring Dad. Please hurry!"

The sound of her daughter's voice sent a shock through Delores, like being plunged into arctic waters. But it didn't make sense, not after the weeks and months of searches, every inch of the forest covered. But then, that sweet lilt of Susan's voice was unmistakable. Images of Susan as a child singing along to the radio in the kitchen while Delores made dinner flashed across her mind. As improbable as it seemed, her daughter was out there, probably not more than a mile away.

"Hank, Hank, come quick! I heard Susan out in the woods!"

Delores couldn't wait as she sprinted across the fresh snow, her chest heaving, hearing Hank behind her, both racing for the chance to hold their daughter in their arms once more.

Delores followed Susan's voice into the forest, the desire to see her daughter so compelling that Delores could almost taste it, and yet... she didn't pay attention to another voice, that of a child's, muffled by the wind; the sound of laughter, sardonic and barbed with pain.

THE SISTERS
Ai Jiang

My father told me that there must not be fear in our village. Whether we are born as girls or boys, we must overcome our fears. Our village has no room for cowards. And no room for cowards, especially within my father's family. He made the same speech during dinners now and then, his gaze boring into me, his booming voice reverberating through our hut. My eyes always flitted away—the intensity unbearable. His voice echoed within me.

My father's eyes reflected the dancing flames in the fire pit behind me. I imagined the flames threatening to jump out and singe my hair and skin, shredding through tissue. It was only, of course, my imagination. I feared too many things—my father could always tell.

But what did my father fear? I supposed he feared nothing, or at least, not anymore. He wouldn't tell me even if I asked him. He always had his fists balled up, as if clutching onto something he did not want others to see.

The longer he stared at me during dinner, the faster the heat rose behind me. I imagined the flames licking the tail of my shirt, burning the fabric, climbing up my back. I shifted in my seat, legs sticking to the wooden chair. When he looked down at his food, concentrating on the sliced chicken in front of him, I felt the flames receding. Rather than burning ashes, I smelled garlic roasted chicken instead; a smell of comfort.

By the end of dinner, sweat drenched my entire back, and I struggled to peel my shirt from damp skin before showering. Never baths for fear of drowning. Once, when I was younger, my father had watched me nearly drown in the lake near our home, until my mother dove in fully clothed and rescued me. She was always fearless when it came to her children.

#

Visiting The Sisters was a rite of passage of sorts, and you couldn't escape it if you wanted to remain in the village. Everyone brought their fears back with them to prove that they'd conquered them. There was a boy who brought back a tiger, slaughtered, on his shoulder. The daughter of one of my mother's friends brought back a serpent wrapped around her body, its tongue absent from its mouth, hanging ajar. My brother never returned from his visit. Most believed he had conquered his fear of death by allowing death to take his life. Yet, my mother often hinted that my brother was alive, somewhere.

#

"Geyuan, tomorrow you'll visit The Sisters," my father said.

The flames brushed the back of my neck. I felt my head bob up and down on its own accord. I wasn't ready. But there was no such thing as readiness when facing one's fears. The villagers said that The Sisters appeared differently to everyone, and you would not recognize your own fears until you met them for yourself, in person.

That night, as I lay awake in bed, I conjured a list of fears in my mind: drowning, death, disease, darkness, poison, pain. When the list grew too long, I purged the thoughts from my mind and squeezed my eyelids together hard, willing sleep to come. I wasn't sure when I had fallen asleep, but when I woke, it was already afternoon.

At night, I would visit The Sisters.

#

The forest near our village always looked welcoming during the daytime, with beautiful rays of sunlight peeking through the foliage. At night, however, the trees seemed to cave into themselves, bending into grotesque angles, making it seem as if the forest was a dense mass of splintered darkness.

My father led me to the edge of the forest, then handed me a lantern and some matches. He told me to walk into the forest without hesitation and The Sisters would appear. But if I hesitated, I would become lost forever.

Is that what happened to my brother, I wondered? Did he become lost like the others?

I pushed the dark thoughts out of my mind. Instead, I heeded my father's warning. I lit the lantern and entered the forest.

My steps were slow but sure. I tried to drive what little confidence I had into the soles and balls of my feet. Regardless, this didn't prepare me for the sight of The Sisters.

The Sisters looked like triplets, with pale skin and stitches sewn through their lips, bound and sealed from top to bottom. They carried sacks made of human skin on gnarled tree branches. The rope—made of strands of their own black hair—crisscrossed the tops of the sacks. Supposedly, the contents of the sacks were different for everyone.

One by one, they walked in a line toward me. Their heads seemed to float above their necks, their sunken eyes spinning under thin, veined eyelids. I feared they might open at any moment.

The Sister in the middle extended a hand toward me. My eyes wandered to her sharp, yellow nails, noticing her hands were made of quilted skin. Icy sweat rolled down my back and collected at the waistband of my pants, and my shirt clung to my skin and cooled far too fast, even with no breeze, only dense, constricting air. The fine hairs on my arms rose, almost in greeting.

When my hand met hers, it surprised me when I couldn't feel the quilted cracks of her scarred skin. Her hand felt seamless, soft—almost fragile. Then her grip tightened, drowning out the remaining warmth of my body. She let go of my hand and moved deeper into the forest.

The others followed her.

I could no longer hold up my quivering body. I swayed, then fell. Crumpled dried leaves pooled around me.

"Come," a voice whispered through the trees. It sounded like the scratching of fingernails on wood with the texture of fresh ashes.

I felt the blood freeze in my veins. I couldn't move. But then I remembered my father's words: *do not hesitate.*

I followed.

#

We halted in a clearing. The Sisters unraveled themselves and formed a semi-circle around me. My breath stalled at midnight, the moon mocking my inability to both inhale and exhale. My knees locked as I tried to stand taller. The Sisters were the same height as me, but they loomed over me, regardless.

One by one, they removed their sacks and held them out. The threads that sealed each sack shut slowly unraveled, as if pulled by invisible fingers. A musty scent drifted from each bag, and I resisted the urge to pinch my nose shut.

"Your fear..." the first Sister said. Her voice croaked like a frog. Her eyes shifted up and down with inhuman speed.

Drowning? Death? Disease? Darkness? Poison? Pain?

The third Sister read my mind and said, "No, no... Not those..."

Their hands moved closer, and with them came the bags.

"Your fear..." said the second Sister.

My right hand hovered above each bag before I plunged into the second one and pulled out what was inside. I wanted to scream, but I knew I mustn't.

The Sisters then disappeared, one by one, in the order they arrived. They left me cowering on the ground, clutching my fear to my chest.

#

It was morning when I awoke. The sun rose high above the treetops and felt warm on my back—reminding me of the heat from the fireplace back home during our dinners. A familiar feeling.

My footsteps were slow on my walk back home, as if my feet moved through molasses slathered on the ground. As I walked, I held my fear in one hand, though I still dared not to look at it.

But the closer I drew to the village, the less afraid I became.

#

The entire village gathered around the arched entrance. High walls stretched around the village for protection. Everyone was waiting for my return.

I saw many hands raise above heads, blocking the sun from squinting eyes. Necks craned forward to see what I held in my hands.

When I finally reached the crowd, everyone bowed to me in greeting—everyone except my father. He stood his ground with his hands clasped behind his back, his chin tilted upward.

We looked alike today.

I walked up to my father and dropped my fear on the ground right between us. Whispers echoed around me, and the villagers took several steps back, each step more hesitant than the next. But not my mother; she stayed close by with an unrecognizable expression on her face.

The villagers all stared wide-eyed at my fear: my father's lifeless eyes staring up into the sky, attached to a disembodied head.

I met my father's gaze, and I could feel the rage dancing in his eyes, escaping and clawing toward me. I smiled a wicked smile upon realizing my father feared fire. He would never sit near the fireplace. I always took the spot instead of him, even though it was the head of the table.

I also realized that this was not a village devoid of fear, it was a village filled with people who hid their fears. The girl who brought back the serpent, and the boy who returned with the tiger—they both left the village for trade. But I understood now they left because the village would only hold them back.

My eyes wandered to my mother, and I noticed her unending strength. How did I not realize that she had only stayed to guide her children after overcoming her own fears? My father had no choice but to stay. He had failed their test. The Sisters' whispers were revealing.

I turned away from both my father and the fear of my father. And as I walked away from the village, I felt the heat disappear behind me.

My brother, I realized, was not dead.

Without a backward glance, I sprinted into the forest in search of The Sisters, knowing my brother would be there.

When I approached The Sisters, they no longer looked as frightening as they did before. Did they ever? Or was it merely the preconceived notions driven into my mind by my father? They were still chilling, but not as terrifying as the others who hide their true selves. Not like my father. I think of the time my father let me drown, the hatred and fear in his eyes. Water. He was also afraid of water.

My brother now stood behind The Sisters with the girl and the boy from the village. They each held out their hands toward me. I walked towards them without hesitation. The Sisters dissipated into the air as I walked through them, leaving the village behind me.

BLISTERS
Scotty Milder

August 1992

The helicopters had been out for days. The *WHAP-WHAP-WHAP* was this nonstop, shimmering drone. It resounded off the granite peaks surrounding the notch canyon that lay between the Ridge and Spruce Mountain.

Sometimes, when he was in the woods beyond the back porch, Dylan looked up and saw the helicopters hovering through the pine tops. A twinkle of light off metal, slashing across a blazing cerulean sky. *Back and forth... back and forth.* Probing. Pursuing.

Dad said the helicopters were from ZOG. At first Dylan liked the word; it sounded all scary and badass, like one of those tentacled monsters he found in all those old Conan the Barbarian paperbacks Dad kept in the back of his closet. But Dad said no, ZOG wasn't a monster. Or not *that* kind of monster. It stood for the Zionist Organized Government, he said. It took Dylan awhile to figure out he was talking about the United States.

Dad said the ZOG choppers were on a recon mission, preparing to launch an all-out assault on the cabin.

Dylan was only twelve. He hadn't watched so much as a news report or a Saturday morning cartoon since before he was eight. But even to him that kind of sounded like bullshit. It was just the six of them out here: Dad, Mom, Uncle Rusty, Dylan, and the twins. And Raider, of course... although Dylan didn't think Raider really counted. It wasn't like he was an attack dog or anything. He was just a scrawny terrier mutt Mom found outside the City Market in Carbondale.

They had some guns, mostly rifles and a few handguns. Uncle Rusty had a sawed-off and a high-powered crossbow, and Dad had the

AK-47 he got off that guy up in Idaho. So why would the Army guys or whatever need to do recon? If they really wanted to, Dylan figured they'd just drive a tank up here and knock the place flat.

Last week Mom said—in that tiny, half-apologetic voice she always fell into when she found herself inching close to a disagreement with Dad—that she thought the helicopters were probably from the news people. They didn't have a TV, not anymore, but it didn't take a genius to figure out that when you shot at federal agents and then battened down inside a cabin deep in the Western Rockies... well, that would probably make a few headlines. Dylan silently concurred, but then Dad told her to stop her stupid cunt lips from flapping and Uncle Rusty damn near busted a gut laughing. Mom got all red in the face. She gathered up the twins and went into the bedroom. So Dylan kept his mouth shut.

Uncle Rusty was with Dad on the whole ZOG thing. Between the two of them, it was *ZOG this* and *ZOG that,* pretty much all the time for the last couple of years. Dylan didn't really know what being a Zionist meant, except that it had something to do with the Jews. Dylan didn't personally know any Jews, but before Dad moved them up here where there was no electricity and they had to trudge out into the woods to take a dump, Dylan used to watch Aunt Beckie's VHS dub of *Spaceballs* and *Blazing Saddles.* Mel Brooks was a Jew. Mel was funny and seemed pretty harmless to Dylan. So he didn't get what all the fuss was about.

Dylan wanted to ask Dad, but Dad talked about the Zionists like whatever was bad about them was self-evident. Like if you didn't know, then you were probably one of them.

#

WHAP-WHAP-WHAP.

Dylan looked up. At first, all he saw were the pines. Their branches—furred with green needles so thick they were almost black—bent upwards and scratched endlessly at that cloudless blue sky.

Then he saw another chopper, making its lazy circle. It was bright yellow, with black stripes along the tail. A news chopper, for sure. Who knows—maybe ZOG controlled the news?

Raider whined and pressed against Dylan's leg. Dylan reached down and scratched the dog behind the ears.

"It's okay, boy," he said, although he was really starting to think it wasn't.

Rusty was up ahead somewhere. They were out looking for fresh game; Mom and Dad and Rusty had spent the last several weeks, before everything went tits up, trying to stock up on food. They dried out strips of elk and venison and bought whatever canned stuff they could at the Price Club in Grand Junction. But the government men showed up with their warrant before Dad was ready. Rusty took a warning shot at them, maybe hit one of them, and now they were stuck up here and supplies were running low. If the siege lasted much longer, Mom said, they were gonna starve. Dylan asked her what "siege" meant, and she said "what's happening now." There was a note of reprimand in her voice that Dylan hadn't heard before. The way she looked at Dad now, it was like there was a thought trying to squirm out of her mouth and she was doing everything she could to swallow it back down.

Yesterday evening, they were sitting around the card table in the big room, eating strips of elk jerky and some sort of canned mush off metal camp plates. Dad and Rusty were playing a listless game of Egyptian Ratscrew. "Fucking tents and shit for miles," Rusty said, reporting back what he had seen earlier that day up on the Ridge. "I didn't see no tanks or nothin', but they're probably on their way."

"Unless they're preparing an air strike," Dad said. "It's what I'd do if I were them."

Rusty cackled. "You ain't smart enough to be them."

Dad glared and played the Five of Hearts. Rusty played the Five of Diamonds, then slapped his hand onto the table and sent his plate flying. Mom picked it up without a word. Her mouth fell open and Dylan held his breath, because he thought maybe she was finally going to let the thought escape. But she didn't. She put the plate with the other dishes, stacked them in the Igloo cooler to be scrubbed off behind the cabin later. Then she took the twins into the bedroom.

That was last night. Mom didn't come out of her bedroom all morning. But when Dylan woke, he could hear her in there. She was trying to shush one of the twins, who was crying. Dad lay snoring on a mat by the wood stove.

Rusty sat at the card table, laying out the cards in a ragged hand of solitaire. He saw that Dylan was awake and tossed him the Enfield rifle. "Come on," he said, and banged out through the back door. "Let's go get some food."

That was an hour ago. Rusty didn't wait for Dylan. He never did. Just disappeared into the trees like a camouflage-clad ghost. Dylan hadn't seen him once since they entered the forest.

He shouldered the rifle and kept moving.

The gently sloping ground gave way to a steep rise. It was all loose shale and a scatter of sharp-faced boulders. Dylan scrabbled up the shale, grabbing at the boulders for balance. Flies buzzed all around him, tasting the salt of his sweat.

Raider bounded happily after him, surefooted as ever.

Dylan got to the top of the rise, where he expected to find Rusty crouching in the brush, waiting for him. Instead, he discovered that he was on a rocky ledge he'd never seen before. It was maybe fifty feet deep and abutted a sheer granite wall. The ledge dropped off to his left into a craggy abyss. To his right, another tumble of shale rose gently into a pine-studded slope.

Dylan craned his neck. The cliff went up at least a hundred feet. Pines jutted all along its jagged top.

He turned back the way he came. Pines rolled away across the valley. The snow-capped peak of Mount Sopris loomed beyond. Dylan knew the highway cut through the trees somewhere between them, but he couldn't see it. He looked to the North, hoping to spy the smattering of buildings that was Carbondale. Like the highway, the town was cloaked by trees. *If it's even there*, Dylan thought. He was gripped by a sudden surety: he'd left Colorado behind somewhere down that slope, had entered the primordial wilderness of Cimmeria.

He turned back to the cliff. He must be on the North Ridge somewhere. He had no idea how he got here or where the hell Uncle

104

Rusty was. Dylan had been looking up at the helicopters and somehow managed to lose his way.

"Shit," he muttered.

Raider ambled forward, head down and nostrils twitching. Dylan studied the cliff. Water oozed from a diagonal cleft maybe twenty feet up the granite wall. It dribbled down the side and gathered in a dark pool that was maybe fifteen feet across.

Something about the pool disquieted him. The surface was black like tar, smooth like glass. It glistened, oily and reptilian, and Dylan found he couldn't tear his eyes away from it.

Years later, when NASA announced it had finally managed to take a picture of a black hole, Dylan stared at the photo—a fuzzy starless eye and an even fuzzier orange iris—and thought back to the pool.

WHAP-WHAP-WHAP...

Dylan didn't look this time. Movement caught his gaze. Raider was trotting forward, following the pool's dusky scent. It was a mineral odor: sharp and bitter, but interlaced with something. Something sour.

A person was lying, face-down, on the edge of the pool.

#

May 2021

A vine-covered hole and a few charred lengths of timber were all that remained of the cabin. Soot blackened the surrounding trees. At some point over the last three decades, someone—a good Samaritan, a bunch of drunk teenagers, whatever, didn't matter—came up here and burned the place flat.

Good, Dylan thought.

He sat in the cab of his pickup truck, drumming his thumb on the wheel and staring at that hole. *Four years.* He had lived here, way off the ass end of nowhere, for *four fucking years.* He tried to think back to that time, but the memories had long since faded—not into the dappled sepia of nostalgia, but into a deep and peaty murk. Mostly what he remembered was the rabbity look in his mother's eyes. The bloodshot glower in his father's. Uncle Rusty's cruel, ever-present leer.

He remembered that last day vividly—although the ensuing years had done much to convince him that what he remembered wasn't exactly possible. The shootout, sure. He still had a few bullet fragments lodged around his right elbow. But not the pool. Not what he found there.

He opened the cab door and stepped out.

The air was cool. Even in late May there was a frostiness to it, so unlike the baking heat of Tucson. He smelled pine sap and mud and a distant carrion stench. Mildew and decay. Dusty, dry death. The smells were like a stick stirring the murk, and another spray of memories tumbled up. Snapshots, mostly. Little vignettes. There were the twins playing in the dirt in front of the cabin, rolling hand-me-down Tonka trucks and making happy *vroom vroom* noises. There was his mother bent over the camp stove, her mouth curled into a grin as she flipped a pancake on a grease-spattered cast-iron skillet. There was Rusty zooming up the road on his ATV, giggling like a crazy person and blasting his shotgun into the air.

And there was the Smiling Man.

The Smiling Man rolled up one day in a plain white Subaru station wagon, maybe three months before the siege. The sound of his car was higher and thinner than Dad's old Chevy. Tourists and hikers turned off this way sometimes, thinking it was a shortcut to the campgrounds up around Twin Peaks or Spruce Mountain. Dad or Rusty disabused them real fast. Usually with a couple shotgun blasts into the dirt.

That day, though, they were all over in Grand Junction. Even Mom and the twins. Stocking up at the Price Club, probably. Usually they made Dylan go with them but, for whatever reason, that day they didn't. He was home alone with Raider, reading one of his dad's Conan novels.

Dylan set the book aside and peered down the road. Raider whined and scrabbled to his feet, tail thumping eagerly against the railing.

By the time the Subaru rolled up to the cabin, Dylan knew it wasn't a hiker or a tourist. He saw the "G" on the license plate. These were government men.

The passenger window rolled down, and a man smiled out at

Dylan. He had a handsome, anonymous face, framed by darkish hair cut with military precision. He wore a greenish jacket and a plain white T-shirt. Mostly what Dylan noticed were the teeth; they were so white and straight they looked fake. Dylan wondered if they were dentures. But the guy was only Dad's age, maybe younger, so the teeth were probably real, bought and paid for from some hotshot big city orthodontist.

"Hey there," the Smiling Man said. "You must be Dylan?"

He framed it as a question. Dylan didn't say anything.

"My name's John," the Smiling Man said, as if Dylan had asked. "I'm here to talk to your dad. He home?"

Dylan shook his head. Raider took a couple tentative steps toward the edge of the porch, his tail whipping gaily. The Smiling Man's grin widened. "That's a nice looking dog. He got a name?"

"Raider," Dylan said, and immediately regretted it. One of Dad's hard and fast rules was that you never—*EVER*—talked to one of ZOG's agents. Don't give 'em anywhere to lay a hook in. You do, and they'll just pull and pull 'til you come apart and spill something.

"Good name," the man said, nodding. "Tell you what, just let your dad know John was here. Tell him we looked into that fella up in Laramie, and things are moving right along. Tell him to give a call as soon as he can. Okay? Think you can remember all that?"

Dylan just stared at him. The man's grin stretched past its breaking point. Dylan found himself thinking about that TV movie he saw when he was a kid, the one where the blond lady got chased around her house by that murderous African doll. The doll had teeth like that.

"Anyway, see you 'round, Dylan. See you, Raider. Good boy."

Raider barked happily. The Smiling Man said something to the driver. The Subaru made a wide U-turn and trundled back down the road.

Afterwards, Dylan found out the Smiling Man was ATF Special Agent John DeSalvo. DeSalvo had been leading the investigation into Dad and Rusty. It had something to do with Dad selling some guns to a couple sovereign-citizen types up in Wyoming and Montana; Dylan never quite pieced together the details. He also never figured out what

DeSalvo meant by "the fella up in Laramie," or what, exactly, was "moving along." He thought maybe it meant Dad was a snitch, or that they were trying to turn him into one.

DeSalvo's face was all over the news for weeks. The pictures were from when he was younger, and they always showed him in his Marine blues. They'd slap that picture up next to Dad's mugshot from that time he punched out the Mexican guy over in Rifle. Dad's photo was all white-red thicket of beard and black, murderous eyes. DeSalvo was a fresh-scrubbed goddamned American hero. Beauty and the Everfucking Beast.

Dylan snapped back to the present. It wasn't 1992 anymore; 1992 was dead and gone, just like the Smiling Man. It was 2021, and none of it meant shit anymore. He looked down the empty road and wondered what he'd do if that Subaru came trundling out of the darkness. If the window rolled down and an eyeless skull with a line of perfect teeth grinned out at him. Would he run? Beg for forgiveness?

You killed my dog, you sonofabitch, he thought.

Then: *You're not here for him.*

A new image floated up, one he'd been trying to keep submerged for nearly three decades. It was an old man's face. Deeply grooved, with skin the color of a walnut shell. Wide, epicanthic eyes. Blood dribbled from the corners. It leaked from slatey gums and smeared across camel-colored teeth. He saw flesh open up in blisters. Skin tore back like flower petals and leaked streamers of blood and pus.

He heard a man's voice, high and raspy, hissing in a language he couldn't understand.

He slammed the truck door on that image, shoving it rudely away. He tossed one last glance down the empty road. The sun was dipping behind the Ridge now, and shadows stretched long from the pines flanking the road. They turned the road into a tunnel, and it seemed to Dylan that staring into that tunnel was like gazing into the rectum of some great, flexing beast. A beast that had swallowed him whole and shit him out the other end—deposited him here, again at the ass end of nowhere, suspended between an unknowable past and a wide, featureless present.

He grabbed the old camper's pack out of the truck bed and turned toward the Ridge. It was crowned in the day's dying light.

Twenty-nine years since Dylan had been up there. He'd gotten lost that day, distracted looking at the helicopters. He had no idea if he could find the pool again.

Didn't matter. The beast had shit him out. There was nowhere else to go.

Time to get going.

#

August 1992

WHAP-WHAP-WHAP...

Raider scuttled forward, tail wagging and nose pressed to the rock. He was headed right for the pool. Right for the person.

"Raider!" Dylan's voice cracked. He chased after the dog, keeping his eyes on the pool. Water dribbled down the cliff face, gathered on a small outcropping where it went *drip... drip... drip* into the pool. Bubbles rose and burst across the surface. *Poison*, he thought. *That water's poison.*

Raider had reached the person and was nudging its downturned face. Dylan noticed two things: it was a man, and that he was missing his legs from the knees down. He lifted a weak hand and tried to push the dog away.

"Raider!"

Dylan dropped next to the man. The man tried to squirm away. Dylan looked down at his legs and felt a ball of vomit bubble into his throat. Wet blue jeans were shredded at mid-thigh. The flesh below the knees was a soupy, suppurating mess. White streamers of fat leaked out of it. Dylan saw muscle and tendon, bone, blood.

The man was still weakly trying to shield himself from Raider's insistent tongue rasping against his leathery cheek. Dylan shoved the dog away and rolled the man onto his back. His skin was slick—either from sweat or from the pool—and exuded a feverish, swampy heat.

Dylan guessed the man was in his sixties. He'd never met an Asian person before—not even when his family lived over in Grand Junction—but he'd seen plenty of pictures. The guy was Chinese or Japanese or Vietnamese or something. His eyes were open. Lips tore back from long, nicotine-stained teeth. A dry, gray tongue flitted around inside his mouth.

"Mister..." Dylan started, then stopped. He tried to think of something to say—something, *anything,* that would help. Nothing came. It was like whatever part of his brain was responsible for making words was stuck on repeat like a scratched CD: *poison... poison... poison... poison...*

The man's lips flapped. He tried to say something. If they were words at all, they were in another language. Or maybe it was just Dylan's broken brain, mixing it all up.

"Mister," Dylan finally managed. "Where'd you come from?"

Raspy syllables poured out of the man. None of it connected to any sound that Dylan recognized. One scarecrow hand reached up and seized the collar of Dylan's shirt. Dylan tried to eel away, but the man's grip was strong and he yanked Dylan forward. A sweaty, rotten stench shoved its way into Dylan's nostrils. He gagged.

"Mister, I'm tryin' to help you!" Dylan yelped. He was vaguely aware that Raider had scuttled off across the ledge, barking. Dylan's mind raced, trying to conjure a solution. He couldn't go to his Dad. The guy wasn't white, which meant Dad was just as likely to shoot him as he was to help him. Same with Rusty. Mom wouldn't do anything. The twins—

—The government men.

Suddenly everything—the siege, ZOG, the guns and the rage and everything else—seemed tiny and unimportant. Dylan didn't care if ZOG was coming to take his freedoms, to murder his race down to the last pureblood white child, to crush all of them under the heels of its vast Zionist boot. All that paled next to *this guy*, this guy who had no business being here, who had tumbled into Dylan's world out of somewhere, hot and sick and maimed. ZOG may be ZOG, or maybe ZOG wasn't even real, maybe was just some crap Dad and Rusty made up. But the government men would know what to do. They would know how to help.

110

"I'm gonna go get someone, okay?"

The man's hand fell away from Dylan's collar.

Raider was over where the shale rose into the pines. Dylan had half a second to wonder what the hell he was barking at when the man suddenly arched his back and screamed.

Dylan leapt to his feet. The man's eyes rolled toward him, imploring. Blood beaded at their corners, dribbled into the grooves of his cheeks.

"Mister—"

The man hissed. Dylan saw more blood gathering along the gums. It smeared across spit-slickened teeth.

The skin across the man's bare chest and arms pulled taut and rippled, as if nests of worms were inside him trying to wriggle free. The skin bubbled into blisters: hundreds of them, pocking out of his narrow chest and abdomen, swelling across his arms and shoulders and hands. They pulsed, almost as one, before rupturing in a unified flood. A smell exploded up at Dylan. Charcoal, meat, sour milk. Dylan gaped as braided ropes of blood and pus sluiced out of the ulcerated flesh, slicked across what was left of the man's dissolving skin in a paste.

The man's lips stretched, then ripped at the corners. His mouth fell open, too wide, as if the hinges of his jaw had shattered. Teeth wriggled out of the gums and thumped back into the bubbling meat of his throat.

Raider yipped. Dylan heard a tumble of rock. He turned, numb, toward the sound.

Two men were making their way down the shale, dressed in heavy green fatigues, their chests and legs covered in black Kevlar. They carried AR-15s clutched high around their chests. Dylan saw patches on their sleeves: "ATF" in gold letters, embossed on black.

The one in front was the Smiling Man. He wasn't smiling now.

"Help!" Dylan yelped, and it didn't sound like a word at all. "Help—!"

But then Raider was shooting forward, barking. Dylan knew that sound, knew it was his *hi friend!* bark. But the Smiling Man didn't know that. His eyes flicked from Dylan to the dog. The rifle swiveled.

Many years later, Dylan tried to remember if he said anything—
"No!" or "Don't!" or "Raider!"—or if he had just screamed. Whatever it
was, it tore out of him like a tangle of barbed wire.

The boom from the Smiling Man's gun exploded off the cliff and
tumbled out into the valley. Raider disappeared in a supernova of
blood and fur.

The Enfield dropped into Dylan's hands before he realized it. The
melting man at his feet was, at that moment, entirely forgotten.

The Smiling Man's eyes whipped back toward Dylan a half second
before the bullet caught him in the throat, just below the helmet strap
and above the top of the Kevlar vest. It didn't so much punch a hole in
the Smiling Man's throat as erase it altogether.

The Smiling Man tumbled, face first, to the shale. Dylan had just
enough time to see the second man aiming his own rifle. He heard
Rusty shouting from up above.

Dylan dove toward the pool. Pain exploded in his elbow, lanced up
his arm like streams of molten silver.

He hit the water.

The world thundered above him.

#

May 2021

Dylan hadn't been back this way for twenty-nine years. The last
time he'd been on Route 133 was in the back of an ambulance.

The second man—ATF Special Agent David Dupeckne—had
apparently pulled him out of the pool, zip-tied his hands behind his
back, and radioed down the mountain for backup. Dylan remembered
none of this. By then, Special Agent John DeSalvo was dead. As was
Uncle Rusty. They told Dylan later he'd been hiding in the trees at the
top of the cliff. When he heard Dylan shouting, he'd come to the edge
just in time to see DeSalvo shooting. He'd shot at Dupeckne with his
crossbow.

Later, Dylan wondered what Rusty had been thinking giving him
the rifle in the first place. Even if they'd come across a deer, the second

Dylan fired, he'd be giving away their position. Like everything else, it was just more evidence that Dad and Rusty really had no fucking clue what they were doing, and were just a couple bumfuck yokels playing commando and making a mess of the game.

Or maybe it meant Rusty didn't give a shit if Dylan got caught, so long as he got away himself.

Or. Maybe Rusty planned this from the start. Was just waiting for an excuse to get a government man in his crosshairs.

Either way, the crossbow missed by a mile. Dupeckne heard the *thwack* of the strings, looked up, and saw Rusty silhouetted against the sky. *Dupeckne* didn't miss. Three rounds, center mass. And, as if that wasn't enough, the fall broke Rusty into about a dozen distinct pieces.

Dylan didn't wake until the ambulance was halfway to Carbondale. His eyes fluttered open to the scream of sirens and he found himself gazing up at a pretty EMT with blond hair and a spray of pink freckles across her nose and cheeks. She saw Dylan was awake, smiled, and Dylan smiled back, wondering how many were dead. Dad? Mom? The twins? Any other government men?

It turned out DeSalvo was the only government man to punch his ticket that day. Dad heard the shots. By the time Dupeckne called for backup, Dad was thundering out the front door with his AK-47. The tanks rolled in. The firefight was short and bloody. Dad took three rounds to the chest, one to the knee, and one to the jaw. Mom was inside the cabin, and she got it in the stomach. The twins were clutched in her arms, and they each took their bullets in the back.

Dylan woke up again in a hospital room. A nurse stood by the bedside, frowning and watching the recap of the whole mess on the TV above Dylan's bed. She never saw that Dylan was awake. He gazed up at her blond hair, all those freckles under the wavering light of the TV, and wondered if she was the pretty EMT's sister.

So that was six dead. Seven, if you counted Raider. Eight, of course, with the Asian man. Who no one ever mentioned. Dylan tried to ask his court-appointed lawyer one time, and the dude looked at him like he was crazy. Dylan remembered the way the Asian man seemed to be melting right before his eyes. *They don't know*, he realized. *They never found anything. By the time anyone else got up there, the guy was just a puddle.*

There was some talk about charging Dylan for DeSalvo's murder, but neither the ATF nor the FBI came out of the thing smelling like roses and, in the end, someone decided it wouldn't be a good look to lay the hammer down on a twelve-year-old kid. The narrative became: *poor Dylan was just as much a victim as Agent DeSalvo, and let's just thank the Lord we were able to at least save him.*

But Aunt Beckie wouldn't take him. Dylan never heard a reason why. So it was the state home for a while, then a spin cycle of foster homes before he ended up with the Beckwiths down in Tucson. Good people. Old. Kinda boring. There were other dogs too: Daisy and Luke and Charlie and Bucket. They were all good dogs. But none was as good a dog as Raider.

And that, as they say, was that.

So. Long story short, Dylan didn't quite remember the way back to the cabin. Nothing looked familiar until he got to Rifle, and even then he only felt the vaguest tingle of familiarity. He hit Carbondale and wound down Route 133. There was Mount Sopris ahead and to the left, overshadowing the pines like some kaiju monster ready to lurch forward and crush everything. Dylan couldn't quite see the Ridge to his right. But he thought he'd be able to recognize the turn-off. It wasn't until Mount Sopris slid past him that he realized he missed it.

He drove up and down that stretch four times, slowing enough that an eighteen wheeler reared up behind him and blatted its horn. Dylan pulled off onto the shoulder, let the truck pass, and kept looking.

Finally, he spied a divot in the trees, a wide spot that may have been a road or may have been nothing at all. He made a U-turn and pulled alongside it so he could get out and take a look.

It was a road, all right: overgrown and carpeted in pine needles, with gnarled trees pressing in. He stared for a long time. The question was: was it *his* road? Would it take him to the cabin, run him into a ditch, or simply dump him off the edge of a ravine?

There was only one way to find out. Luckily, his pickup was four-wheel drive. He didn't really need that down in Tucson, but right now he was glad to have it. He inched off the highway and onto the road. Inside the canopy of trees, it was so dark it was almost night. He turned on the high beams and listened to the crunch of needles beneath his tires. The truck crawled forward, first angling down (*this can't be right, the road didn't go DOWN, did it?*) before finally leveling off and starting to rise. He kept the needle at five miles an hour.

Eventually, he came to the hole. The burnt timbers.

He was home.

The result of all this was that by the time he climbed out of the truck, the sun was going down. Night had oozed into the woods like an oil slick. Dylan knew he should set up camp and try to find the pool in the morning. But the thought of camping *here*—where *all* of them died—sent shivers up his spine. At least by the pool, Uncle Rusty would be the only ghost.

That thought brought a flash of bleeding gums, an agonized and unintelligible hiss, the wet sound of teeth plopping into flesh.

No. Not the only ghost.

He gazed toward the Ridge, which was now just a deep blackness against the sky. *You'll never find your way*, he thought. He was only there the one time, and by accident.

And yet... somehow he thought the way would find him.

Dylan had a big LED Maglite buried in his pack. He dug it out and got going. He took his time, letting the beam sweep over tree trunks and roots that curled out of the ground like tentacles. The crunch of his boots upon the pine needles was obscenely loud in this reverent darkness. He kept expecting to hear the far-off hoot of an owl, or the distant yip of coyotes. Maybe even Raider barking somewhere way up the Ridge. But there was nothing.

There was no sense of place or orientation; only the steady sense of *rise* told him he was heading in generally the right direction. He kept looking up, hoping to see something that jogged his memory: a tree split from lightning, or an irregularly shaped outcropping. But it all blended into an impressionistic canvas of texture and muted, shadow-splashed color.

You'll never find it this way, he thought. For all he knew, he was drifting further and further away. He resolved to stop at the next flat spot he found, set up his tent in the dark, and try again at first light.

Almost as soon as that idea entered his mind, the flashlight landed on a boulder. The quartz embedded in its pockmarked surface glittered madly under the beam.

He tilted the light upward. It crawled across another boulder. Then another. *Another.* The ground between them was loose shale, angling steeply upward. He trained the light as far as it would go. The shale ended abruptly somewhere above him. Beyond was a perfect, churning darkness.

There was no way to know for sure if this was the spot. These woods were lousy with rock-strewn hills like this. But he stared into that black void at the top and somehow he *knew*. There was a malingering presence up there, the crush of something watchful and waiting.

The shale skidded under his boots as he climbed. Every time he lifted one foot to take a step, the other threatened to slide out from under him. He went slow, keeping the flashlight aimed, as best he could, at the slope ahead of him. The beam jittered in his trembling hand.

It'll be dried up, he thought. *There won't be anything there.* Maybe a shallow depression where the ledge met the cliff, rubbed smooth and clean from rainwater.

But halfway up, he could smell it. That acrid, mineral stench.

He climbed faster.

#

Splash.

At first, Dylan didn't know exactly where he was. For a moment it seemed to him that an enormous snake had gotten into his apartment—maybe slithered up the fire escape and crawled through his bedroom window—and was sucking him into its slick and dilating gullet. Then he realized it was just his sleeping bag.

It came back to him in fits and starts; he dimly remembered

getting to the top of the slope and gazing dully as the flashlight beam shimmered off the surface of the pool, which seemed to stretch on all sides into blackness. He remembered setting up his tent and crawling into his sleeping bag as exhaustion crawled out of that blackness to claim him.

Splash.

Then: a sob.

A fist of terror plunged into Dylan, seized hold of his heart and squeezed. His breath thudded out of him in a rattling gasp. Black spots exploded behind his eyes.

Home, he thought. *I want to go home.*

A high, keening wail followed the sob. A girl's voice cried out: "... help... help me!"

Dylan shoved the sleeping bag off himself, then unzipped his tent and crawled outside.

The flashlight's beam slid across the rocky ledge, wavered over the surface of the pool. Again, he saw bubbles pushing up from below.

Then the light landed on a wide, upturned face. Red-yellow hair fell in lank streamers across pale cheeks. Braces glinted in the hard LED light.

"... help me!"

Dylan hurried forward. Déjà vu slammed into him as he dropped to his knees. He almost thought he could hear Raider panting beside him, the sound of a wet tongue rasping against wrinkled skin.

He shoved the flashlight into his belt loop, snaked his arms into the girl's armpits, and dragged her away from the pool. The same pungent, rotten-milk stench poured off of her. The same febrile heat baked out of her skin. The flashlight beam jittered over the cliff face and bounced back down on them and he saw that she was wearing a bathing suit. It was one piece, polyester, pink and blue with what looked like flowers embroidered around the hips. He guessed she was sixteen or seventeen.

"You're okay," he said through gritted teeth, and noticed with zero surprise that her left leg was gone from mid shin. A chalky sliver of bone jutted from the glistening stump.

The girl was panting. He lay her on her back and brushed the hair away from her face.

"Mom," she gasped. "Where's my mom?"

"I don't know."

"Where am I?"

Dylan didn't want to answer that just yet. "You're okay," he said again. "What's your name?"

"K... Kelcey. Where's my mom?"

"She's coming," Dylan lied. "She's on her way. Can you... can you tell me what happened?"

"I don't know," she moaned. "Where's my—?"

Her breath cut off with a sudden, strangled yip. Her eyes fluttered, then rolled over white.

Dylan patted her cheek. "Kelcey. Stay with me, okay? Your mom is on her way. And, uh... we've got an ambulance coming. But you need to stay with me. Can you tell me where you are?"

"P... Pelican Lake," she said.

"Good. Where's that?"

She looked up at him, eyes snapping in as she really saw him for the first time. "You're not a lifeguard," she said.

"No. Where's Pelican Lake?"

"*Wisconsin.*" Her tone was almost affronted.

"Can you tell me what date it is?"

"Huh?"

"The date, Kelcey. What day is it?"

"I... don't know. May something."

"Good. What year?"

"*Huh?*"

"Kelcey, what year is it?"

"Twenty twenty one. What the hell?"

"Good, Kelcey. Real good."

He sat back, pulled the flashlight out of his belt loop, and aimed the beam at her. Her leg was a mess, but otherwise she looked okay. He knew she wasn't, though.

Her eyes were glassing over. "I want my mom," she whimpered.

"I know. She's almost here."

"My leg hurts."

"I know. We've got help coming."

"Where am I?"

"You're on the shore of Pelican Lake," Dylan said. "In Wisconsin."

Her head rolled toward him. Her eyes glittered wetly in the flashlight beam. She squinted against it. "No, I'm not," she said.

He sighed and clicked off the flashlight. "Okay," he said. "You're on the side of a mountain in Colorado."

"What?"

"Kelcey, can you tell me what happened?"

She squeezed her eyes shut and grimaced. Her breath hitched, made a damp rattle in her chest. "We were... on the boat. Out on... the lake," she said. "Dylan—"

"What?"

She opened her eyes and looked at him.

"My brother Dylan. He was... horsing around with... the... the soccer ball. Being... an asshole. Mom... told him... told him to stop. He... bumped into me and... and I..."

Her eyes fluttered. She was going into shock.

Dylan again patted her cheek. "Kelcey, stay here with me, okay? Your mom will be here real soon."

"No... she won't..."

"What happened after you fell in?"

"... Colorado..."

"Kelcey, what happened—?"

"Light," she said.

Another cold fist wrapped around Dylan's throat and squeezed.

"Light?" he croaked.

Her face relaxed, so sudden it was like watching a film strip run past with a few frames missing. She turned her gaze toward the sky and smiled.

"There was a light..."

... and a rifle BOOMS. *Rusty is shouting somewhere high on the cliff above.*

A hot ball of pain slams into Dylan's elbow. He hits the water.
BOOM! BOOM BOOM BOOM!

Dylan thrashes. The pool sucks him down. He tries to kick, but the water resists him, dances nimbly away and then wraps long, greasy fingers around his calves. It pulls.

He opens his eyes onto a blackness that goes forever. It swirls into his nostrils and throat, itches across his eyeballs. There's no bottom to it.

He should be drowning, but realizes that he's not. Because it's not water anymore. Whatever this space is, it's limbic. Liminal. A cold, enveloping nothing.

He kicks.

Light swells out of the nothing. It starts as a pinprick, then fattens, distending, warping the essential flatness of this space into something three-dimensional, then four, then five, then... then... then...

Dylan drifts toward it. Not down or up. Just toward. It bulges like a jellyfish. Tendrils snake from it into the darkness like solar flares. If there's a color to it, he can't make any sense of it.

It whispers, not in words exactly, but a soothing, gentle purr. He knows what it's telling him.

Come, *it says in his mind.*

Something irises open at its center. Dark flowering upon light. A deeper black than he ever thought imaginable.

Through, *it says...*

From somewhere: BOOM! BOOM! BOOM!

No, *Dylan thinks.*

And pushes away.

#

It didn't take her very long.

Dylan didn't bother trying to comfort her. What could he say? Her mom wasn't coming. There were no ambulances.

He thought about asking her: *what was it like?*

But by then she had nothing left to offer but screams. He sat there, cross-legged, and watched her skin burst open. Watched it belch out ribbons of pus and fat and liquifying tissue. Watched steam rise from the open cavities, noxious vapors twisting into the night.

At the very end, her eyes rolled toward him: wide, terrified, never once acquiescing or giving in. Then they popped like grapes and sizzled into the melting caverns of her face.

Within twenty minutes there was nothing left but a scattering of teeth in a tacky, red-blown lacquer. Fifteen minutes after that, the teeth were all that were left. He picked one up and turned it between his thumb and forefinger. It was a molar, the silvery filling still embedded in its center. He pitched it off the ledge, where it tumbled into the night.

He wondered if, right now, there were divers in Pelican Lake, looking for the body.

The sun was just starting to come up behind him, purpling the sky and inking shadows all along the cliff face. He looked at the pool. It was black. Still, except for the water trickling down the cliff face.

Drip... drip... drip...

This was what you wanted, Dylan thought, although he wasn't sure that was true. He wanted proof, sure. Wanted to know the nightmares that plagued him all his life were rooted in something real.

It knew you were coming, he thought. *It knew you were coming, and it gave you a gift.*

So, what are you going to do with it?

Certainly not dive into the pool, kick down into that nothingness until he saw the light—light that wasn't light at all, not really, but a blister on the surface of reality.

You've got an apartment back home. A decent job. A foster brother and sister who love you, even if they never really say it. Bucket's in the kennel, waiting for you. There's even that cute-as-shit bartender down at the Bay Horse, the one with all the tattoos who lights up every time you come in. Even the door guy said she's into you.

He could go back and live that life. Live it like he hadn't once killed a man for shooting his dog. Live it like the government hadn't gunned down his entire family. Live it like there wasn't a pool way up here on a Colorado Ridge surrounded by pine trees—a pool that wasn't really a pool at all but a... what... a portal? A tear across the fabric of everything rational?

Part of him wanted to dive into it. He really did. Just to know for sure. He'd wash up, missing a leg or two, in Vietnam or Wisconsin or Switzerland or maybe in the deep oceans of Europa. His flesh would melt away as he lay there screaming.

But maybe—just maybe—it would be worth it.

He thought about it. For a long time.

"Fuck it," he muttered finally, and stood. "It'll keep."

He went to his tent, crawled inside, and zipped the flap shut behind him.

PIGFOOT
Daniel Barnett

"**H**arlow wasn't** a coal town back in those days. It was a slaughter town, and the men who couldn't wear a tie carried a knife to work. Stickers, they were called, and the best of them was Harold Comlin. Harold could carve a thousand throats in one day, and not get a drop on him. He *loved* those pigs, was greedy for them. Other guys, they'd crack jokes and have smoke breaks every chance they got, anything to lighten the mood, but not Harold. He liked to be alone in the kill room for hours, just him and his pink little friends. He'd whisper to them, scratch their stubbly ears, and all the while his knife would go flick, flick, flick. To Harold Comlin, the sweetest sound in the world was a squeal."

Jerry Michaels yawned. He was bored. These days he was always bored, unless he was angry. "Thought you said this was a scary story."

"It is," said Lloyd Friendly, "and it's *not* a story."

"Just shut up and listen," said Lloyd's sister, Sasha. It was dark inside the bedroom with Lloyd's chubby face hogging most of the flashlight's beam, but Jerry was pretty sure Sasha winked at him. Not that he cared. Much.

Lloyd cleared his throat and resumed his tale-teller's voice, which was fuller—more robust—than his real voice. He wanted to be a director when he grew up, and he was probably framing this moment as a movie scene in his head: the three kids huddled in darkness, the creaky old house settling in around them, the moonlit track leading through the woods outside...

"It was the summer of '88 that Old Betsy shut down for good."

"Old Betsy?" said Jerry.

"The slaughterhouse. They named her like she was a boat."

"Then you should have said she *sunk*."

"But Old Betsy didn't sink. She burned." Lloyd pushed his round glasses back up his nose. "That summer was hot even for Kentucky, and dry. My daddy, he was a kid then, and he says that summer nobody sweat. You couldn't finish swallowing your water before you were thirsty again. There was dust everywhere dust wasn't meant to be—you had to wipe down the table before every meal, and rinse your hair in the morning because the dust would climb right into bed with you."

"Your daddy said all that?" Jerry asked with a little smile. The Friendlys' country ways were still new to him. Back in New York where he'd come from, twelve year old boys who called their dads 'daddy' suffered a short life expectancy.

"Most of it." Lloyd shrugged. "Some of it."

"Will you stop interrupting my brother?" said Sasha.

"Will your brother get to the point? Hot summer, dry summer, so what?"

"*So*," Lloyd said, "there wasn't anything to stop that first spark once it set into the hay bales behind Old Betsy. No one knows for sure where the fire came from—there were clouds that day, and some swear they saw dry lightning flickering after dusk. The hay, though, that had been brought in for the pens so the pigs would have something to lay on. The flames spread fast. They licked up Old Betsy, gobbling at every part of her that wasn't brick, and soon they found their way inside. To the meat. A fresh shipment had just come in, two thousand some swine all packed in and waiting to be stuck. There wasn't nobody in Harlow that night who didn't hear the squeals. But it was Harold Comlin who answered them fastest. He couldn't stand it, hearing those pigs screaming, knowing the fire was having all the fun. He ran into old Betsy with his knife and no shoes on, he was so excited. No one saw him alive again. One day later when the fire died, the wind came up and carried ashes from Old Betsy's husk. At last enough blew away and they found him, his clothes burned, his blade still in hand. The pigs had escaped their pens, and he'd killed them by the hundreds, buried himself in them, their blood cooked black on his skin, their flesh and fat molded to his feet from every step he took over their melting bodies before he finally fell."

Lloyd let the image hang over them in the dark.

"It's been thirty years now, but on some nights you can still see him out there, trudging through the slaughterhouse in search of another throat to cut, his lumpy pink feet dragging on the ground. They're not quite human anymore, those feet, and they're not happy either. That's how you know he's coming, by the sound they make, that's how you know Pigfoot's coming... *squee... squee... squeeeeeee...*"

Lloyd snapped off the flashlight. A scuffle took place between he and his sister, during which Sasha somehow managed to relocate herself next to Jerry's bed. Jerry felt a cool finger run up his legs in the dark, and then the overheads turned on—stabbingly bright. His father stood in the doorway, wearing an apologetic smile underneath sad brown eyes. Lucas Michaels looked like someone waiting for bad news. He'd looked that way as long as Jerry could remember.

"Mr. Michaels, you scared me!" Sasha said, clutching Jerry's calf to cover up the tickle she'd been giving it.

"I'm very sorry," said Jerry's dad, and Jerry thought that about summed up his old man. Very sorry. Jerry wondered how long he'd been listening in on them. They had moved to Harlow two months back after budget cuts in education caused his dad to lose his teaching job in New York, and his dad was already moving around this rangy old house with ease, as if he'd been here his whole life. Meanwhile Jerry couldn't take a piss in the night without barking his shin on something. It wasn't fair. None of it was fair.

"What's up, Daddy?" he said. "You have a bad dream?"

"It's almost one," Lucas said. "Time to pack up the campfire stories and turn in. And Sasha..." He nodded to her sleeping bag. Her parents had given three justifications for letting Sasha sleep over at a boy's house: Mr. Michaels was a teacher, her brother would be in the same room, and the 'boy' in question was twelve, not thirteen. Whatever *that* meant.

Sasha finished segregating herself on the other side of Lloyd, who squirmed down into his sleeping bag. Jerry's dad reached for the light switch. Paused. "You know, maybe he didn't do it for fun. Your Pigfoot. Maybe he went in there to save those pigs, and when he couldn't, he killed them out of mercy so they wouldn't have to burn."

The lights turned off. The door shut. Jerry listened to his dad's footsteps retreat quietly to the upstairs bedroom. "What a bastard," he said, not realizing until he spoke that he wasn't joking, that he was actually mad. "He has to find the softness inside everyone. He can't even let a monster be mean. Even a stupid monster like Pigfoot. Everything's got to be a tragedy, a misunderstanding, boo-fucking-hoo." Jerry thumped his head down onto his pillow. He sat back up as if launched. "And screw you guys, too. You told me I was going to shit myself over your story, and it wasn't even scary at all. *Squee, squee, squee,* you can both go suck one."

Sasha spoke in the dark. "You only say that because you haven't heard the best part yet."

"What do you mean?"

"How do you think Harold Comlin got there so fast, the night old Betsy burned?" She was smiling. He could hear it in her voice.

"I don't know. Roller skates?"

"He lived close, he and his son." Lloyd now. "When the fire started, he could see the glow from the kitchen window."

"Wait. Pigfoot had a son?"

"Sure. Kid named Kyle. About our age."

"What happened to him?"

"Got sent off to foster care, I think," said Lloyd.

"Where he spent the rest of his childhood getting diddled and doodled," added Sasha.

"That's gross, sis."

"That's foster care."

Jerry swung his legs off the bed. "So what? They lived close to the slaughterhouse. How's that supposed to scare me?"

"He hasn't figured it out, Sash."

"No, he hasn't. He's pretty slow. You want to tell him?"

"You tell him. I told the rest of the story."

"It's supposed to scare you, Jerry, because—"

"Because you're living in his house!" said Lloyd. "You and your dad are living in Pigfoot's house!"

There was a muffled thump that might have been a punch to the arm. "Hey jerk, you said I could tell it."

"You were going too slow."

"I was building suspense."

"The suspense was already built. You were just dragging it out."

"Was not."

"Sis, sis, listen. I know this stuff. I study it. I'm going to write and direct my own movies one day."

"You couldn't direct traffic if you were a street sign."

"Tell her, Jerry. Tell her she was dragging it out... Jerry?"

Jerry was thinking. About his frown of a father. About home so far away, and his own unhappiness, always close. A next door neighbor to his heart. "The kitchen window faces the same way as my window."

"Yeah," said the male Friendly.

"That means the slaughterhouse is that way, through the woods." Jerry stared outside to the moonlit track leading into the dark trees.

"Yeah, down a path, I think."

"Well, what are we sitting here for then? Old Betsy's waiting. Let's pay her a visit."

The room hushed at Jerry's suggestion. Then Sasha's face appeared over the flashlight, pale, nervous, excited. "For serious?" she said.

"For serious."

"No hood no," said the bolt-upright shadow of her brother. "That's a stupid idea. That idea is how you die."

Jerry laughed. "What, you don't *really* believe in Pigfoot, do you?"

"No! I mean, Harold, he was real, but—"

"What then? What's the problem?"

"It's dark, and that's the problem. And that place is dangerous—there's barbwire all around Old Betsy, just to keep stupid people out."

"We'll just take a peek. We won't go inside or anything. Come on, I'm new to town. You're supposed to show me the sights."

"Tomorrow. In the *day*."

"Now."

"Your dad told us to go to bed."

Funny how dads were only 'daddy' when they were your own. "My dad is a wimp. He won't even know we're gone, and if he did find out, if, he'd probably apologize to *us*."

"You don't have to come, Lloyd," Sasha said, her blue eyes on Jerry. "Me and J will go alone."

"You just want a chance to stick your tongue down his throat."

"Shut up."

"He's a *city* boy, and you just think that's oh-so cute."

Another Friendly scuffle took place on the floor. Jerry stepped around their struggling bodies, went to the window, and climbed out quietly into the warm night. "Who's coming?" he said.

Sasha was coming, and in a hurry. She straddled the windowsill in her pajamas—her rather tight pajamas—and landed next to Jerry with the flashlight.

"Oh hell." Her brother rustled out of his sleeping bag and got to his feet.

"Wait," Sasha stage-whispered.

"What?"

"Get our shoes. We can't go without shoes. What are you, an idiot?"

#

Trails are like humans in at least one way. They need to feed to survive, and the trail to Old Betsy had not been fed in a long, long time. Untrodden in decades, the path had starved, thinning from a packed lane to what was little more than a crack in the dense wall of the woods. The three kids followed it single file, Jerry in the lead and Lloyd in the rear, his shoulders hunched up to his ears. Witchgrass tickled at their ankles. Branches clawed at everything else. They forced their way deeper, the glow of their flashlight pocketed by the trees, the full moon playing peekaboo through the stitchwork overhead, a pale sliver here, a bony slice there.

And then, under that same moon, Old Betsy.

She did not announce herself. She did not need announcing. She stood alone on stage under her spotlight where she had always stood, like a forgotten starlet waiting for her audience to return. Her dress was as red as the blood that had once been spilled inside her; the bricks were blackened by char, torn down, and sewn back together in places by lacy green threads of ivy. Wind hooted owlishly through her open mouths. She sang a sad song, Old Betsy. She had sung it for many nights, and she would sing it for many more.

Jerry stared up at her from the edge of the clearing. He'd gotten through the woods a few paces ahead of the others, and it couldn't have been hard to see for Sasha since she was carrying the flashlight, but she still managed to bump into him. She didn't exactly *un*-bump herself either.

"Wow," she said, attached to his side. "Creepy."

"Whatever," he said, and he wasn't playing cool. He was bored, and annoyed with himself for being bored when he should have been something—anything—else.

Sasha took his hand one exquisitely cool finger at a time. He thought about letting go. He thought about it some more, and decided he would. Not now, though. In a few seconds. A few at the most.

"Well, there's your peek," said Lloyd. He must have been saving his voice for a scream because he hadn't spoken since leaving the house. "Can we go now, please?"

"You said there was barbwire." Jerry waved an arm. The clearing was bare except for foxtails and a few boulders growing moss over ancient burns. "There's not even a fence around the place."

Lloyd sighed. "Wishful thinking."

"You mean you've never been here? After all that talk?"

"Well..."

"He hasn't," said Sasha, a shadow of awe—or fear—in her voice. "Nobody comes here. The road to Old Betsy—you can't see it because it's on her other side, her front side—the road cuts through the woods, and they let it go just like the path from your house. Now there's just a couple of green ruts with baby trees growing all around them. This place is shut off like Dracula's castle up in the mountains. The people in town all whisper about it, but half of us don't really believe it exists."

"And Pigfoot, he's the Count?"

"Pigfoot is dead."

So was the Count, technically, Jerry thought about saying. Instead he nudged Lloyd with an elbow. "You listening, pal? Your sister really set the scene there. I'm practically shivering. I think she should get the director's chair when you two grow up."

"Screw you."

"No thanks. I'm saving myself for someone special."

Sasha's hand tightened on his, but Jerry couldn't say if that was in response to him or to the low, mournful note rising from Old Betsy. The slaughterhouse seemed bigger. Closer. Good thing the moon was out, or they wouldn't even know she was there, and what if they heard her singing then? What if they heard her singing to them from the dark *then*?

The thought was enough to give Jerry a chill, and for a moment— for the first time in a long time—where he was didn't feel so far away from where he wanted to be. He was *here*. He was *here*, and it wasn't fair, but maybe it was all right. Jerry searched the hole inside him, the one that was made when he was forced to leave behind his friends in New York for this Nowhere on the middle of the map. The hole no longer seemed quite so deep, so full of echoes. Then the chill faded and the anger came back freshly cooked. Anger at nothing, at everything, but most of all anger at his father, who didn't care. And that was the root of it, wasn't it? His father didn't care. Sure, he looked sad. He looked like he'd been hung up on the cross, like all this was so hard on him, but he never once asked how it was on Jerry. He couldn't even *see* Jerry past himself. Hell, he probably wouldn't notice if Jerry never came home tomorrow. Not until Mr. and Mrs. Friendly came looking for *their* kids.

"Fuck it," said Jerry. He was grinning broadly. His eyes felt ten degrees too hot in their sockets. "Let's go in. Let's see if Count Pigfoot is home."

He let go of Sasha's hand and headed off without waiting for an answer, leaving them no choice but to follow or abandon him to Old Betsy and whatever waited inside.

#

Lucas Michaels lay awake in the bedroom that had once belonged to Harold Comlin, the man whose death had given birth to Pigfoot. He couldn't sleep. He rarely could since returning to this house. God knew he'd had his share of nightmares here, back in the days when the slaughterhouse was still in operation, when Old Betsy was just Betsy and he was an eleven-year old boy named Kyle, listening to the squeals of her tenants through his window at night.

They never stopped crying, those pigs. Not until they met the knife.

Lucas turned on his bedside lamp. He rubbed his face, which was the face of a man pushing forty except for the gray hairs on his cheeks and the distant—some might even say sorrowful—look in his eyes. The gray had come in before his beard finished growing. The look in his eyes had been there much longer.

Lucas poured himself a drink from the bottle in his nightstand. Bourbon. Kentucky blooded, just like him, though Jerry didn't know that. Jerry didn't know a lot of things about him, and that was for the best. No boy deserves to carry the sins of his father, especially when the sins were as heavy as Lucas's. He'd been born the son of Harold Comlin, and he'd gone to school the son of Harold Comlin. The kids at Harlow Elementary used to sing jingles to him about his old man. *Slice, slice, they squeal so nice.* Or, *Stick 'em, lick 'em, slip your prick in 'em.* Eventually the worst had happened. Lucas had begun to believe their rhymes. He'd begun to see the monster everyone else saw in his father, and then...

Lucas downed his drink. The bourbon hit his stomach like a lit match, but the fire died down after a while, as fires almost always do, and left him feeling hollowed out and burned. He walked to the closet in the slow way that he had walked through the last thirty years. On the top shelf was a shoebox, which he had kept with him since moving in with his aunt and uncle in Nashville. He had lived with them until he was eighteen, at which point he'd taken their last name, Michaels, and done away with Kyle for good. Jerry knew them as Grandma and Grandpa, and they were more than fine with that, having no actual children of their own. This house had come to them in the will, and they had held onto the deed in case the time should ever come when Lucas wanted to return to Harlow. That time never did, but the time where he *needed* to had. Lucas hadn't told Jerry, didn't want him to worry, but the two of them had been a breath away from being homeless in New York, and so he had manufactured a little white lie. A job opportunity at a middle school in the country, where teachers were in high demand and the cost of living was cheap. Only one person in town remembered him. Ms. Beauford, the principal of Harlow Junior High, where Lucas worked and where his son went to school. Ms. Beauford had roosted there since time immemorial. Before Lucas's aunt had taken him in, before she had married and become a Michaels, she herself had sat at a desk in Ms. Beauford's class, she and her quiet, sensitive brother, Harold Comlin.

Lucas took the shoebox down off its shelf and carried it to bed. He hadn't gone through the box since Jerry was born, but he had never stopped adding to it over the years. *Oh, son, I hope you never have a box like this one. I hope you never need something to hide all your hurt... and your guilt.*

He lifted the lid.

Inside were newspaper clippings and pages printed off the internet. The newest additions sat closer to the top, covering the old. Lucas took out the first. It was of a fire. All the items in the box were of a fire. This one had taken place in 2012, four years ago, at the Harlow liquor store. The owner had made the unknowing mistake of kicking on his old genny after a power outage killed electricity on the block. The genny blew, and before long things were hot enough in Harlow's Sips that the bottles of Bacardi 151 and Absinthe (legal now and high enough in alcohol content to be set aflame) were popping like fireworks. Being a stubborn old fool, the owner had made several trips into the burning store to save his higher shelf inventory. On his last rescue mission, he had seen someone pacing the back aisle of the store: "Just a shadow, a big, shouldery shadow, walking behind the smoke." The owner had called out, but he'd barely been able to hear his own voice over the glass cracking, and the mysterious figure had marched out of sight, never to be seen again.

Lucas searched the fire in the photograph. The flames were so bright they rendered everything around them blurry. He saw nothing.

The next article was dated 2006, and featured the heading: *Eight Dead after Explosion.* Someone had tapped into a gas pocket down in the coal mine, and a wall of burning air had rushed through the tunnel, incinerating everyone in its way. All of this was rather unextraordinary, though tragic, except for the testimonial given by the only survivor, who had been caught behind falling rock and saved from the explosion. This man swore that in the minutes following the blast, he heard footsteps in the tunnel. Heavy, slow footsteps. He himself pointed out that this was impossible—the tunnel had been full of boiling smoke, airless, and anyone able to draw breath wouldn't have been doing so for long, let alone walking around. "It was probably just my head," he told the Harlow Herald. "My head had been pounding something awful."

Lucas agreed. It had probably been the man's head.

Probably.

He pulled out the photograph of a charred two-story house. The owner had forgotten to put on the fire screen before falling asleep on the couch in the den, and he had woken inside Hell—everything hot, crackling. On his way out the door, his arm over his mouth (this detail Lucas inserted himself; he had visualized this story more than once), the man heard what he thought was his infant daughter wailing upstairs. He didn't know that his wife had already carried the little girl from the house and was holding her on the front lawn in tears. Dad followed the squealing up to the baby's room, only it didn't sound like his daughter up there, or any other human he had ever known. It sounded like an animal. Animals. When he opened the door, the squealing stopped. A man stood over the crib. A large man with a long knife that glinted in the firelight. The man turned. There were flames all around him, on the walls and in the crib, consuming the twisted blanket where the daughter had lain. There were flames everywhere but on the man, and yet his eyes burned. Red, flickering. He took a step, dragging one foot through the smoke rising from the floorboards, and that was all the father remembered except for the squeals that seemed to chase him from the house.

Lucas set aside the article, which had been published on a paranormal website titled *PigfootWalks*. There were other supposed sightings of the legend, most of them reporting huge body counts that THE MEDIA IGNORED! There was even a paternity claim: WOMAN RAPED BY PIGFOOT GIVES BIRTH TO SWINE. But the story of the burning house Lucas believed, partially because of the fire, partially because the father had grown up outside of Harlow and had not been weaned on its myths.

Lucas went through the remaining pages one by one, going back one fire at a time through the town's history. Not all of the articles hinted at anything unordinary, but many came with at least one peculiar footnote: an out of place sound or the feeling, for those involved, of someone nearby in the flames. Someone glimpsed but never seen again. Someone looking... searching...

"For another throat to cut," Lucas said, and then shook his head. No, not that. He didn't believe that.

At last he came to the bottom of the box. To the worst, if not the original, fire to ever grace Harlow. There were two photographs. In the first Old Betsy burned beneath a dark sky, where low clouds boiled orange and sweaty, soured red. In the second photo was a small boy whose name had been Kyle and whose face, underneath the ash, might have belonged to Lucas's own son.

Lucas brushed the boy's grainy black cheek, thinking of Jerry, and shivered.

It was like touching a ghost.

#

The chute down which pigs had once been fed into the mouth of Old Betsy remained upright after all these years. Its switchbacks stood shiny black in the moonlight, like a line at a deserted amusement park. Eerie... but also inviting.

Jerry hopped the railing. A bit of soot smeared onto his palm when he landed, and he absently wiped it away on his shorts as he waited for the others to catch up to him. Sasha did first, followed a moment later by the walking "no"-machine that her brother had become.

"No no no no, just no."

"Let's go back," Jerry inserted.

"No no—wait—"

"Too late, you had your chance." Jerry headed down the chute. The ground was handpicked and ruggedly uneven, and he knew why as soon as Sasha's flashlight flicked after him. They were walking over ancient hoofprints, tramped into the mud and fossilized there. They were on the path of the soon-to-be slaughtered, and oh boy, that thought should have terrified him, but it didn't. It exhilarated him. He wondered if his dad had known about Old Betsy before moving to Harlow. Probably. Perhaps that's why they'd gotten the house so cheap. Urban legends were terrible for the real estate market.

"Thanks Pigfoot," he muttered.

"What?" said Sasha.

"Nothing."

They exited the final switchback and started for the slaughterhouse's entrance. It was wide open. There'd been a door once, like the kind on a garage, but the whole frame had collapsed during the fire. A pile of blackened beams and corrugated sheet metal lay off to the side, cleared away and left to rot with the rest of the building. Jerry paused in the doorway, testing to see what he felt, standing where no one had stood in years or even decades. Unless Dracula's castle was not empty... unless a certain squee-ing Count lived within these walls.

The answer was not much. A little colder, maybe. Old Betsy's song was not just a sound here, but a real thing. Her cool breath tickled the exposed hairs on his legs. He could hear her bones groaning softly. He could see—and the realization stopped him. He could *see*. Old Betsy's roof had been made of timber, and as a result most had been eaten away. The moon peered down through great jagged rifts, paling all it touched and leaving the rest in shadow.

"I'm not going in there," said Lloyd, licking the cleft in his lip. He and Sasha were twins, but the dice had rolled badly for him in their mother's stomach. Lloyd got crooked teeth. Sasha got a Hollywood smile. His hair was frizzy. Hers was smooth and straight. And that didn't even take into account the prepubescent acne, or the extra rolls equipped to his stomach. No, the house had not favored Lloyd

Friendly. "I don't care if Sasha gets pregnant, I really don't, I'm not going in there."

"Yeah, sure, whatever you say."

"I'm serious."

"Okay. See you inside."

"No, you won't."

"Okay."

"Okay."

Jerry walked into Old Betsy and was surprised as well as disappointed when Lloyd stuck to his word. Now there was no one left to protect him from Sasha. He stole a glance at her. "You scared?"

"Yeah." Except she didn't look scared. Anxious, maybe, but not scared. "You?"

"My pants are loaded with shit."

"Ew."

They were moving between what used to be the pens. Bits of chicken wire were all that remained of the fences. The pens' floors looked black and crumbly, and back in the corners where the wind and rain didn't have access, there were dark lumps that might have once been pigs.

"Do you smell that?" said Jerry.

"If you're still talking about your shit, you can stop."

"No, really. It smells like... it smells like... bacon."

"Ha. Ha." She elbowed him. Then a bone crunched under his foot, and the joke didn't seem that funny any more.

"What would they call us?" said Sasha.

"Huh?"

"If there was something that ate us, what would we be called?" High walls, reaching up toward the threadwork roof and sky above, gave way to the low stone ceiling of a corridor as they passed beyond the pens. "Pigs are pork. Cows are beef. Birds are fowl. What would we be?"

Jerry shrugged.

Sasha was quiet for a moment. "Folk," she said. "They'd call us folk so they wouldn't have to feel bad about eating us. There'd be restaurants serving folk fillet, and folk liver pate, and kid meat would be called something fancy and sophisticated to make it sound like a delicacy."

"Adolescencia."

"Too long."

"Adol. Like the singer, kind of."

"Yeah. Adol. Served rare. With a glass of pinot noir."

"Delicious." Jerry gave his hand a nibble and regretted the choice immediately. He still had soot on his palm.

It was hard to see under the low ceiling, and they were forced to rely on the flashlight to find their way. Where were they now? Jerry wondered, listening to their footsteps click off the stone. Some passage, it seemed. One last chute between the pens and wherever the knives came out to play. A pale curve glinted in the dark overhead. A hook, dangling from a retractable chain attached to a steel track in the ceiling.

"Shine that up a bit, will you?"

Sasha lifted the flashlight. More hooks hung overhead, one every few feet. "Fun."

The hall ended, and the track continued into a closed circular space. Not too large. Cozy, almost, except for the railway of hooks running along the wall. The floor was grated, and the gaps in the grates were so wide Jerry felt as though he were walking on solid darkness. The kill room. This was where the pigs came to be cut. They trundled in on the track, hanging upside down from their ankles, and batch after batch they went on, bleeding from their throats, into a square hole set high in the wall. If there was a Pigfoot, they would find him here.

Jerry cupped his hands to his mouth. "Halloooooooo."

His voice came back to him in the same hollow tune that Old Betsy sang her song. "*Hallooooooo.*"

The castle was empty.

Dracula was dead.

Disappointment welled inside him. There was nothing to be afraid of here. Like his father's tragic revision of Harold Comlin's death, Old Betsy was just depressing. At least Sasha hadn't tried to make out with him. He'd kissed a girl before, once, but his friend Joaquin from New

York told him that country girls were like preacher's daughters, clean in public but dirty in private, and what if Sasha wanted to do *more* than kiss? Last week Jerry jerked off in the shower, thinking of Rooney Mara, and it hadn't worked right. Well. It had felt good for a second, really, really good, and then... there was no 'and then.' All the guys at school talked about grabbing for tissues so they wouldn't bead themselves in the eye. The way they told it, they all had firehoses down there. But for Jerry, nothing. Not a single drop. He could live with being broken if he had to, maybe, but no way was he running around third base and falling on the way to home plate. *No way.* He'd rather die.

"What now?" he said, but got no answer. He turned. "Sasha?"

She was sitting on the grates, her legs crossed, looking down into the flashlight. The beam lit up her face—and it was not such a bad face to have lit up, Jerry thought—so that the worry there was plain to see.

"What's wrong?"

"Nothing," she said. "I just thought it'd be different. That I'd feel different. When we were outside, when I saw Old Betsy for the first time, I told myself she was creepy—because how couldn't she be?—and I got the willies for a second. But they didn't stick around and so then I thought if I went inside, if I just followed you inside..."

"You'd get scared?"

"Yeah. But that's not it. Not all of it. I wanted to show myself *what* to be scared about. I wanted to find something to scare me for real, so I could teach my head to see things straight. Lloyd, this place is real for him. He didn't need to see Old Betsy because he already built her up inside of him with those stories. But me, you know what I was thinking when we walked through the pens?" She looked up at Jerry, and her eyes were painfully blue. "I was thinking my legs look fat in these dumb sweats, and how's that for stupid? I'm in a slaughterhouse, and it's night, and there are dead things everywhere, and I'm still not *here*. My head's still saying, *Sasha, you shouldn't have eaten that sandwich for dinner, there was so much bread on it, Sasha, your love handles, Sasha, your thighs.*"

"Your legs aren't fat," Jerry said after a moment. "Your legs are really nice."

"That's not the point!" she shouted, making her voice bounce around the kill room. "It's not about what they are or aren't, or what you think. Your opinion doesn't fix the way I feel. Nothing does, because there's something wrong with me, and *that's* the problem."

"I just thought you were trying to impress me, coming here."

"Not everything's about you."

"So you weren't trying to impress me?"

"Well..." She smiled, and of all the unfair things in the world, the most unfair was how pretty that smile made her.

Maybe Jerry was a little scared, after all. Maybe he'd only been angry because he didn't miss New York quite as much as he used to, and the pain of losing something you loved was easier to hold onto than the pain of letting go of it completely.

He held out his hand. She took it, and neither of them let go once she found her feet. A light sweat came to Jerry's brow despite the cool air circulating through the kill room. They started back the way they had come, and yes, he would admit it, he was scared. Terrified. Her fingers locked between his. Her thighs brushing his own. His heartbeat pounded so loud in his throat and head that at first he didn't hear the soft, steady sound coming toward them from down the corridor. *Squee... squee... squee.* Like pigs under the knife. Like pigs to the slaughter. *Squee... squee... squeeeeeeee...*

A pair of red-orange eyes flickered brightly in the dark.

A husky, burned voice whispered, "*Kyle?*"

#

The worst thing in life was not realizing you were loved, not knowing you were home, until it was too late. Lucas Michaels set down the picture of himself as a boy, the picture that so closely resembled his son, and packed his collection of fires back into the shoebox. When he finished, the cardboard felt almost hot to the touch, but that was only his imagination. The children's bedtime story had gotten the wheels of his mind spinning, and they wouldn't stop now until they carried him to the end of memory lane, which for Lucas—now and forever—was the path leading to Old Betsy through the woods.

Slice, slice, slice, they squeal so nice.

Lucas had listened to the rhyme so many times through elementary and middle school that it might have been the anthem. Kids in the halls would sing it to him as they passed. He would open his locker to find the jingle written on the door in red permanent marker. Girls would run away from him oinking and squealing, and once a rumor that he had brought his father's work knife caused the teacher to root through his bag in the middle of class, in front of everyone. But worst of all were the rhymes he'd dream up in his sleep, little variations of the original that offered darker, uglier insights into his father, fears that Lucas would not even admit to himself. *Squeal, squeal, squeal, they make me real.* Or, *Squeal, squeal, squeal, I cannot feel.* In these dreams Harold Comlin was a ghost who grew more solid with each stroke of his knife, becoming not human but monstrous, a hunchbacked and bloodied mailman, laughing as he delivered his pink screaming bundles to Hell. They said his father was the reason his mother skipped town. They said he couldn't love anything unless it was upside down and hanging from a hook.

And Lucas (then Kyle) believed them.

He became jealous of the pigs, of the attention they commanded from his father. In the stories told, his father crooned to them, as if singing them to sleep. He gave them smiles and pets and he stroked behind their ears, while at home he was quiet, distant, always looking somewhere far off. Food was on the table every night, and new clothes and school supplies came to Kyle when needed, but he only ever got part of his father, never the whole thing. Old Betsy held onto the rest.

And so, on a cloudy night in the particularly dry summer of '88, Kyle paid her a visit. He snuck out after his father fell asleep and stole down the path behind the house, carrying the matchbook that sat on the hearth over the fireplace. He told himself he was saving his dad, freeing him from the slaughterhouse before it spoiled him completely, but in truth he'd been trying to save himself. From the torment of school. From the lonely, angry kid he was becoming.

He knew about the hay bales because his father had paid for them out of his own pocket, so that the pigs would have something soft to lay on in their pens. It never crossed Kyle's mind that this little act of kindness might explain the stories surrounding his father, that every song, every soft touch and smile, was Harold's way of making the pigs as comfortable as possible before he fulfilled the unspeakable duties of his job, the only job a simple man like Harold Comlin could get in a slaughter town like Harlow. Kyle never thought of the pigs once as he lit the match and held its flame to the lowest hay bale. They were just a part of the slaughterhouse and its architecture, no different than the bricks in the walls or the timber in the ceiling.

Until the fire took hold.

Until the pigs began to scream.

It started as a low, confused muttering inside Old Betsy—a groggy conversation that built into a noise as bright and terrible as the flames grappling up the woodwork. The clouded night sky glowed like a bottle full of angry fireflies. The temperature climbed. Kyle backed away from the hay bales, now a burning pyre that reached thirty feet high. Sweat poured off his face in rivers. The hairs on his arms twisted and curled from the raw heat. His eyes were wide and stinging, but he could not close them, could not look away from what he had done... and what *had* he done? Oh God, what had he *done?* Old Betsy crackled. Her roof spit and popped. Against the seething brightness of her, Kyle must have been a dark spec, almost invisible. Which explained why his father didn't see him standing there, behind the slaughterhouse.

Harold Comlin came to the clearing wearing his nightshirt and work pants, nothing else, not even shoes. He had woken to the sound of squeals and struggled into the denim jeans lying on his closet floor, his work knife still hooked to the belt. Stepping out of the house, seeing the violent glow over the woods, he had forgotten all about the boots on the porch and he had run. At least that was what Kyle told himself later, fitting together the missing pieces of the story. There was one question he never could answer, though, one question that haunted him above all others, and that question was: What if he had not seen his father coming out of the woods? What if he and his father had passed by one another unknowingly, like ships in the night? Would children today still whisper about Pigfoot?

It didn't matter.

Because what happened was this:

Standing behind the slaughterhouse, in shock at what he'd done, Kyle caught a movement in the corner of his vision. The movement was his father, running around Old Betsy. Kyle followed him in a slow, dazed walk, and when he saw him again, his father was standing by the chute, staring up at the burning building with a look of horror and sadness. There were flames reflected in his father's eyes. Finally, Harold Comlin made a decision. He opened the gate. He ran inside.

Kyle wanted to follow him, but the doorway to Old Betsy was so bright. So *loud*. Her smoking mouth howled a thousand squeals.

He could not say how long he stood there waiting for his father to return, only that with each passing moment, the hot coal of his stomach grew hotter. Every nerve in his body was a blade; his skin was a network of knives, whittling him down and down. At last something emerged from the slaughterhouse, and another something, and another. The pigs trampled through the chutes, running for the first time in their history with Old Betsy, away from Old Betsy. What the newspapers only mentioned in passing, and what the tales of Harold Comlin never mentioned at all, is that over three hundred pigs escaped the flames that night. For a full month after the fire, you couldn't step outside without seeing a hog wander by on the road or root around a dumpster. They wandered into backyards and got fed by kids. They drank water left out in dog bowls and slept under porches. Most were rounded up and slaughtered eventually, but not all of them, not all, and that was Harold Comlin's *true* legacy:

He saved a few.

He did what he could.

The flow of pigs slowed to a trickle, and at the back of the stampede was Kyle's father, stumbling, his nightshirt pulled over his nose and mouth. The tops of his feet were black, blistered. Sparks fizzled out in his long, dark hair. His eyes had closed to squinting lines, and tears rolled from them, leaving clean tracks in the soot on his cheeks.

Kyle was so relieved to see him that he called out: "Dad!"

There's a reason that fire codes require emergency exits to lock from the outside, and that is because people who have inhaled enough smoke will sometimes become confused and go back into the burning building from which they have already escaped, thinking they are still inside.

At the sound of his son's voice, Harold Comlin's face registered bewilderment. He must have believed Kyle to be at home in bed. The bewilderment became terror. He turned to Old Betsy. Then he went inside, staggering drunkenly, the knife on his work belt shining firelight.

The doorway to the slaughterhouse collapsed behind him.

Kyle tried to dig his way through, but the pieces of wood burned his hands. He heard his father searching for him, calling his name. He heard pigs squealing inside the oven of the slaughterhouse. He heard them squeal as he would hear them squeal for the rest of his life, in the dark chute of his dreams. And he heard by their punctuated grunts when his father began to cut their throats. Perhaps they were simply in his way, but Kyle didn't think so then, and Lucas didn't think so now. No. Even while searching for his son, Harold Comlin had been doing what little he could for them, as he had been doing his whole life.

Lucas put the shoebox back on its shelf. His hands were trembling, the scars on them a reminder of the terrible price he had paid to learn of his father's love. He hadn't said a word to anyone that night, not to the firemen who found him pawing at Old Betsy's burning front door or the policemen who later questioned him, and he never told anyone of the matchbook he had taken from the hearth over the fireplace. The only person he had something to say to was his father, but for that he'd never have the chance.

He walked downstairs. It was cooler there, and he needed cool. After going into the kitchen for a glass of water, he went down the hall to his son's bedroom. Not a sound came from inside. The kids were fast asleep. He started to turn when he remembered... Jerry had stayed over at the Friendly house, and had come back a tired wreck because Lloyd wouldn't stop snoring. With a frown, Lucas opened the door.

The bedroom was empty.

143

Through the woods, through the open window that had belonged to him as a boy, came a sound from Lucas's childhood.

Squeals.

Human squeals.

From the slaughterhouse.

#

"Kyle?" said the man, who was nothing more than a pair of firelit eyes in the dark. There was a note of recognition in his voice, and that Jerry could not handle. It surpassed his brain's ability to process. He began to shake, not only his arms and legs but his middle too, like his spine was a fault line.

He wasn't shaking alone. The flashlight rattled in Sasha's hand, and as the eyes floated closer, growing brighter, its beam revealed the man's body in pieces. A broad set of shoulders clung to by charred rags. A face cooked down to the skull. A thick hand whose fingers had been welded together, closed permanently around the handle of a long knife. Feet like charred globs of bubblegum. Feet that stuck wetly to the ground, and stretched with every step... and *squealed*, though they had no mouths to speak of, only folds of dripping pink skin.

Pigfoot.

Pigfoot was real, and he was coming.

They fled back into the kill room, holding hands tighter now than ever. The grates pounded and groaned beneath them. Everything was either dark or it was a hook, glinting briefly, cruelly, as the flashlight swept around in search of an exit.

Squeee... squeeeeee... squeeeeeeee...

"There." Sasha dragged Jerry toward the hole in the wall where the railway and its hooks disappeared. "Help me up," she said, letting go of his hand to grab the lip of the opening. He tried to push her, lift her, but his arms were full of air. He was a balloon boy, floating away. Jerry began to laugh. They were scared now! Oh boy were they scared!

Sasha slapped him.

The sting in his cheeks killed the helium valve in his chest. He got his hands together, got her foot in his hands, and shoved her up into the hole. The squeals were getting closer. The kill room sounded as it must have sounded in the days when Old Betsy was still alive.

Sasha set down the flashlight, and Jerry took her hands in the dark. He climbed the wall, his feet sliding on the burned stone, and then he was crawling after her on all fours, like a pig in a chute. Above them the hooks rattled gently on their chains, tinkling like evil wind chimes. A draft carried down the narrow passage from somewhere up ahead.

Sasha screamed, and Jerry heard her fall an instant before the rough stones gave way to nothing beneath him. He landed on her a few feet down. His neck cracked. He tumbled and stopped on his back, looking up but not seeing anything. They had forgotten the flashlight.

"Jerry? Jerry, are you okay?"

"I think so."

"Where are we?"

He tried to piece everything together, put it all in order. The stone corridor. The kill room. The passage that was just big enough for dancing pigs to pass through... what came next? What came next? His fear was a huge, clumsy thing, plodding over his thoughts. "I don't know. I don't remember."

Up ahead something glimmered softly. Not a hook. Those were much higher in this place. No, this glimmer belonged to something bigger, fuller, something whose side was rounded gently, like the wall of a massive pot. "The boiler! They boil them, then they break down their bodies." Jerry got to his feet (Sasha had already found hers) and they set off in a panting shamble that was very much like a crawl.

Above the boiler some of the ceiling had crumbled, leaving the railway and its hooks intact but letting in a shaft of cold moonlight. Jerry had never seen anything so pure, so beautiful. "Follow the tracks. Follow the tracks, and they'll lead us out."

The next room was bright by comparison. The ceiling had caved in completely, having lost the support of its wooden beams, and here the pig's railway finally ran its course. Amid the fallen stones sat steel flaying tables, and the crude instruments that had once been put into practice on them. They staggered over the stones, making small landslides with their footsteps. Sasha looked as though she had been rolling around inside a spent campfire, and Jerry's skin felt coated in grime. Somewhere along the way the fingers of their hands had intertwined again, and she dragged him in excitement as a plain metal door came into sight. They had reached the end of the path. Past this point would be the pens, the entrance, the woods, *home*.

The door wouldn't open.

Sasha pushed and pushed, but it gave no more than an inch. Jerry shoved her aside and threw himself against the metal. Something groaned but did not budge on the other side. The door was blocked.

"Look for another way out."

There was no other way out. The walls stood twelve feet high, too high and slippery to climb. Jerry's eyes caught on a slot in the stone up above the flaying tables—there were so *many* of them—but his heart quickly sank. The slot was far too narrow to fit them; it must have been where the railway began its journey back to the pens after dropping off the dead pigs for disassembly. This was the last stop in the ride, and they were trapped. *Think. Think.* There had to be parts of the bodies that the flayers threw away. The pigs came into the slaughterhouse in a chute, and what was left of them would have exited the building in another chute, a garbage chute, but where, where, where?

The answer came to Jerry, and he wanted to cry.

The stones. The fallen stones. Whatever way out there might have been, the collapsed ceiling had buried it.

"Do you hear anything?" said Sasha.

He listened. "No."

"Me neither."

"Maybe he couldn't fit through the passage. Maybe he can't get in here."

But even as he spoke the words, he knew them to be a false hope. Pigfoot was dead, and this was his castle. From the other end of the flaying room came a soft squeal, followed by another, another, another.

Jerry and Sasha clutched each other.

And screamed.

#

Lucas stood at the window of his son's bedroom, listening to the screams from Old Betsy. He knew who those screams belonged to. Even if he hadn't been able to recognize Jerry's voice, crying out in terror, he would have known. Things always came full circle. His father had been here, in a moment much like this, listening to squeals from the slaughterhouse. Squeals of his son's making. Now it was Lucas's turn, and he had a choice, but his decision first depended on a simple question:

Did he believe in Pigfoot?

Yes. Yes, he did.

And because he believed in Pigfoot, there was really no choice at all. He could run through the woods to Old Betsy as his father had run, but he would never find them in time. Not in the dark, and not in his father's domain. The path through the woods would only end in sadness and slaughter.

His mind made up—no, his heart; this was a matter of the heart—Lucas walked back down the hall to the living room. The fireplace was cold with winter a long ways off, but there was a box of matches above the hearth. Lucas shook out a handful. As a boy he'd only needed one, but he was taking no chances. He went quickly, calmly, to the office where he kept all of his lesson plans. He took a stack of old papers, crumpled a few into balls, and set them on the windowsill beneath the drapes. Then he lit the crumpled pages. As flames climbed the curtains, he carried the stack of papers into the living room, going from the windows to the couch to the sofa chair, leaving a little fire at every stop.

Let this work.

For my son, for his friends, please let this work.

#

Squeal by squeal, Pigfoot came. His walk was the walk of the burned, the suffering, the slaughtered. Jerry understood this even as he screamed. He heard—felt—Old Betsy singing her sad song all around, and it came to him that they were a part of that song now, their voices her voice. And he knew how terror and tragedy could become so deeply intertwined it was impossible to tell the two apart. Fear and sorrow woven together like the fingers of his hand, Sasha's hand. He'd never kiss her now. They'd never make fun of Lloyd and his movies again. They were going to die. Pigfoot was coming. They were going to die, and the dying was going to hurt so, so bad. His footsteps promised that.

Squeee... squeeeeee...

When the next squeal did not come, they kept screaming. For a long time they kept screaming, unable to stop, unable to believe in the silence that had fallen over the flaying room. The door shuddered open behind them. They fell backwards onto dirty ground.

Lloyd looked down at them. "Jesus, you two, how'd you get stuck in there?"

"Pigfoot," said Sasha. "Pigfoot. He chased us."

"Ha. Ha. Very funny."

"No. No. He's real."

"Sure he is, sure, and you can tell me *all* about him as we leave. Seriously, haven't you guys had enough of this place for one night?"

They had, and after they all hopped over the charred beam that Lloyd had shoved away from the door, he was struggling to keep up with them as they ran through the moonlit pens. Jerry kept expecting a shadow to rise from the floor and fix them with burning eyes, but Old Betsy stayed still. Her horrors had gone back to sleep for the night, or else...

Jerry didn't know what else.

The way outside came into view ahead. He started to cry, and by the time they reached the chutes, the open sky above them, he was sobbing. Sasha was too. He grabbed her and kissed her, a big, clumsy, wet kiss on the mouth. Lloyd groaned.

Jogging, laughing between sobs, they went around Old Betsy. There, behind the slaughterhouse, they stopped.

The sky over the woods glowed an angry violet.

Jerry's house was on fire.

#

"You came."

Lucas faced his father in the burning living room. The curtains were fiery wraiths, twisting, curling, as if in pain. The couch was a smoking pit. Scorch marks spread across the crackling walls and ceiling. The bare floorboards were hot and growing hotter by the second. The only place untouched by heat was the fireplace.

Harold Comlin plodded forward in his death suit. His naked skull peeked through the charred flesh on his head. His eyes reflected new flames, old flames. This was how he saw the world, Lucas knew. This was the hell he had been sentenced to. An undying inferno, where everything and everyone burned. Where the only salvation was his sticking knife.

Squeeee, squeeee, squeeee. Harold's feet dripped like candle wax as he walked. Like lard. Lucas could smell the sweet stink of pork rising off him. Beneath the rags of his nightshirt, his skin was black with cooked blood, pig's blood. His jeans were holey, the flesh beneath seared to a crisp so that it crinkled and split with every step he took. Lucas looked up at him. He was older now than his father, but standing before him he was still a boy.

Pigfoot's lipless, cracking mouth shaped a word. "*Kyle?*"

"Yes, Daddy. Yes, it's your Kyle. You found me." Lucas's voice broke. "I'm sorry. You've been looking for so long. I'm so sorry."

Flames licked at Lucas's calves. Flames climbed the sleeve of his shirt. But he did not move. He reached up and cupped his father's ruined face. There were tears in Harold Comlin's blazing eyes. They shimmered orange-red in the light.

"*Kyle.*"

"Daddy, I'm burning." It was becoming hard to find words, to focus. "Daddy, it hurts."

Pigfoot hugged his son. Tight. The knife slipped in between the shoulder blades and stopped at the hilt. Blood dribbled from Lucas's mouth. He smiled. The fire didn't seem so hot anymore, all of a sudden.

"We're home," he said. "We're home."

They held each other in the flames.

#

Jerry reached the house first, and through the living room window, through the smoke, he saw his father embrace Pigfoot. A moment later, the gas line exploded, and they were swallowed in the fire.

Sasha and Lloyd arrived at last.

They had to hold Jerry back to keep him from running inside.

#

Lucas Michaels' body was bagged up by morning, and because no one had reason to suspect anything other than an accident, what was left of him went unexamined to the crematory, where he was turned to ashes according to his will. News of his relationship to Harold Comlin broke soon after, and a new chapter was added to Pigfoot's legend. All this information Jerry took in and processed quietly, along with the other facts of his new life.

He moved in with his grandparents (except they weren't really his grandparents) in Nashville, which was a two hour drive away from Harlow depending on traffic. Mr. and Mrs. Friendly brought their kids to visit him every other weekend, and he was grateful for that, though he didn't say so.

Lloyd bought a new video recorder with three years of allowance money, and he showed Jerry the home movies he made on the Michaels' small box-screen television. He still didn't believe they'd seen Pigfoot that night, but he promised to make it all into a great movie one day. If, that was, Jerry didn't mind.

Sasha never talked about Old Betsy or what had happened there, and that was all right. She and Jerry spent a lot of time kissing. That was all right, too.

Jerry had nightmares for a few months, but never of the slaughterhouse or the march or squealing footsteps. His nightmares were always of the same thing: his father standing at the bedroom door.

"I'm very sorry," his dad would say, and Jerry would reply, "What's up, Daddy? You have a bad dream?" Then he would wake, shivering, and hug his pillow until sleep came again.

In December his grandmother (Jerry had decided she really was his grandma after all, whether or not she had been his father's mom) knocked on his door and entered the room. She held a little box wrapped in reindeer paper. She said, "This belonged to me and your grandpa, but we thought you should have it since... since there wasn't anything left."

Jerry waited for her to go before opening the box.

Inside was a framed photograph of his father as a young man and Jerry as a kid, small enough to be hooked in one arm. He was pulling his father's hair and his father was laughing, no frown to be found on his mouth or in his eyes.

"You set that fire, didn't you, Dad? It wasn't an accident. I know it wasn't."

If Lloyd ever made his Pigfoot movie, Jerry knew there'd never be a quiet ending like this, with a boy holding onto an old photograph. But Lloyd thought this was the story of a monster, when, really, it wasn't. It was a story of fathers and sons.

About the Authors

Daniel Barnett, author of "Pigfoot," is a lover of stories—especially the scary ones. He has four published novels and is currently hard at work on the Nightmareland Chronicles, an ongoing serialized adventure horror epic following one man's journey to reach his daughter in a world claimed by eternal night. You can find his books on Amazon or chat with him on Twitter at @dbhfiction.

Douglas Ford, author of "Ladders," lives and works on the west coast of Florida, just off an exit made famous by a Jack Ketchum short story. He is the author of a recent collection of weird fiction, *Ape in the Ring and Other Tales of the Macabre and Uncanny*, as well as the novel, *The Beasts of Vissaria County*, due out from D&T Publishing in 2021. His short stories have appeared in such venues as Dark Moon Digest, Tales to Terrify, Weird City, along with The Best Hardcore Horror, Volumes Three and Four. His novella, *The Reattachment*, appeared in 2019 courtesy of Madness Heart Press. Follow him on Instagram at instagram.com/author_douglas_ford/.

Amelia Gorman, author of "Giant Killer," lives in Eureka where she enjoys exploring the forests and tidepools with her dogs and the many rescue-dog fosters who come through her house. You can read more of her fiction in *Nox Pareidolia* from Nightscape Press and her poetry in Vastarien, Star*Line, and Liminality Magazine. Visit her website at ameliagorman.com or follow her on Twitter at @gorman_ghast.

Scott Paul Hallam, author of "One Red Shoe," is a speculative fiction writer living in Pittsburgh, PA. His work has been published in *DreamForge Magazine; Sanitarium Magazine; 100 Word Horrors Book 3, Switchblade Magazine*; and Unnerving's *Hardened Hearts* anthology, among others. He earned his Master's in English Literature from Duquesne University and first fell in love with the written word when his dad read him stories by Edgar Allan Poe as a kid. Follow him on Twitter at @ScottHallam1313.

Ai Jiang, author of "The Sisters," is a Chinese-Canadian writer, an immigrant from Fujian, and an active member of the HWA. She draws on cultures and landscapes of the lands she has walked for inspiration. Her work has appeared or is forthcoming in F&SF, The Dark, Dark Matter, Hobart Pulp, among others. Find her on Twitter @AiJiang and online at aijiang.ca.

Scotty Milder, author of "Blisters," was born and raised in Los Alamos, New Mexico, the birthplace of the atomic bomb. He began publishing short stories in indie horror magazines while in college, and went on to earn an MFA in Screenwriting from Boston University. He has developed screenplays with independent producers and major Hollywood studios, and his low-budget feature film *Dead Billy* is available on Amazon, Google Play, and other streaming platforms. His short fiction has appeared or will appear in Dark Moon Digest, Lovecraftiana Magazine, the Scare You To Sleep podcast, and anthologies from Sinister Smile Press, Dark Ink Books, Little Demon Books, and others. You can follow him online at scottymilder.com.

S.R. Miller, author of "Red Moon Lodge," hails from the Midwest, but formative years playing Oregon Trail have led him to make the slow journey west, where he has somehow avoided dying of dysentery. Along with writing, his love of the arts has taken many forms, including playing guitar in heavy metal bands, and working with an indie game company. Author of the horror novel *Sweet Dreams for Laura*, he and his wife now call Oregon home. Follow him on Facebook at facebook.com/srmwriting.

Maggie Slater, author of "Circles," is a speculative fiction author hailing from the woods of New England. Her fiction has appeared in *Zombies: More Recent Dead* from Prime Books, The Bronzeville

154

Bee, and Apex Magazine among other venues. She enjoys Haruki Murakami novels, sampling craft beer, and hoarding cheap notebooks. Visit her website at maggiedot.wordpress.com.

Originally from Texas, **Mark Wheaton, author of "Ghost Forest,"** started out as a writer on horror movies like *Friday the 13th* (2009), the Sam Raimi-produced *The Messengers*, and the Emilia Clarke-starring *Voice from the Stone*. In 2016-17, his three-book crime trilogy about a priest solving mysteries in Los Angeles came out from Thomas & Mercer. His first sci-fi novel, *Emily Eternal*, arrived from Grand Central Publishing in 2019 and was named one of the five Best Science Fiction Books of the Year by the Financial Times. His next book, *The Quake Cities*, arrives in 2021 from Severn House. He has also written for video games and co-created the Dark Horse comic, *The Cleaners*. Visit his website at mark-wheaton.com or follow him on Twitter at @Mark_Wheaton.

About the Editor

Aric Sundquist is an author of speculative fiction and owner/editor of Dark Peninsula Press. Born and raised in Michigan's Upper Peninsula, he graduated from Northern Michigan University with a Master's Degree in Creative Writing. His short stories have appeared in numerous publications, including *The Best of Dark Moon Digest*, *Night Terrors III*, *Daylight Dims*, *Fearful Fathoms Vol 1*, and *Attic Toys*. A writer and a musician at heart, he also enjoys board games, guitar, and traveling. Currently, he lives in Marquette, Michigan, with his girlfriend Elsa, and a ferocious beagle named Bruce. You can visit his author website at aricsundquist.weebly.com.

Dark Peninsula Press
The Cellar Door Anthology Series
www.darkpeninsulapress

Other titles by Dark Peninsula Press:

Negative Space: An Anthology of Survival Horror

Violent Vixens: An Homage to Grindhouse Horror

Serious Applicants Only: A Horror Comedy

Made in the USA
Middletown, DE
28 October 2022

13632590R00096